⚜ THE ⚜
Strictest School
IN THE WORLD

⚝ THE ⚝
Strictest School
IN THE WORLD

Being the Tale of a Clever Girl, a Rubber Boy and a Collection of Flying Machines, Mostly Broken

By Howard Whitehouse

With illustrations by Bill Slavin

Kids Can Press

To the original Emmaline, cleverest of cats — H.W.

Kids Can Press acknowledges the financial support of the Government of Ontario, through the Ontario Media Development Corporation's Ontario Book Initiative; the Ontario Arts Council; the Canada Council for the Arts; and the Government of Canada, through the BPIDP, for our publishing activity.

Published in Canada by
Kids Can Press Ltd.
29 Birch Avenue
Toronto, ON M4V 1E2

Published in the U.S. by
Kids Can Press Ltd.
2250 Military Road
Tonawanda, NY 14150

www.kidscanpress.com

Edited by Tara Walker
Designed by Marie Bartholomew
Printed and bound in Canada

CM 06 0 9 8 7 6 5 4 3 2 1
CM PA 06 0 9 8 7 6 5 4 3 2 1

Library and Archives Canada Cataloguing in Publication

Whitehouse, Howard

The strictest school in the world : being the tale of a clever girl, a rubber boy and a collection of flying machines, mostly broken / written by Howard Whitehouse ; illustrated by Bill Slavin.

ISBN-13: 978-1-55337-882-2 (bound) ISBN-10: 1-55337-882-2 (bound)
ISBN-13: 978-1-55337-883-9 (pbk.) ISBN-10: 1-55337-883-0 (pbk.)

I. Slavin, Bill II. Title.

PS8645.H565S77 2006   jC813'.6   C2005-907669-0

Kids Can Press is a /©r∪s™ Entertainment company

CONTENTS

DRAMATIS PERSONAE

Emmaline Cayley
A Pioneer of Aviation

Rubberbones
A Bouncing Boy

Aunt Lucy
The Best Sort of Aunt

Lal Singh
A Mysterious and Heroic Butler

Josie
Wields a Dangerous Stick

Princess Purnah
A Royal Personage from a Distant Land

Mrs. Wackett
A Horrifying Headmistress

Professor Bellbuckle
A Mad Inventor

Miss Scantcommon
A Monstrous Matron

Miss Sharpelbow
A Terrifying Teacher

Sid and Norah
Romany Travelers

Stanley
An Enthusiastic Dog

A FEW INTRODUCTORY REMARKS ABOUT A BOSSY QUEEN, UNCOMFORTABLE UNDERWEAR AND MISERABLE WEATHER

This is a story about a world gone by. A place of wonder and fantasy and weird inventions. A place where science and strange new ways of doing things collided in a heap with ancient beliefs and strange old ways of doing things.

We call it the Victorian Age, although everyone at the time called it "now." It started in London, England, in 1837, when a young princess named Victoria became queen, and carried on until she died at a very great age in 1901. Since she was not the sort of old lady you'd want to argue with, it carried on without her for another few years. This was the time when the British Empire stretched over many parts of the world, shown as red areas on a globe (the actual places weren't painted red, as that would have been messy). Even people from countries that weren't ruled by Queen Victoria knew who she was; quite often she was their own ruler's aunt or grandmother. Even the Americans, who'd gone to a lot of trouble to be rid of kings, held Victoria in great respect, though none of their presidents were related to her at all. That's why old American houses are sometimes referred to as being Victorian, though she was never actually queen there. (I'm not sure anyone had the nerve to tell her.)

Got all that, then?

And the people were pretty much the same as the ones we know. Except that their underwear was much more uncomfortable.

So, let's head off to a land of make-believe, of astounding inventions and unspeakable horror. A village in Yorkshire, England, with a funny name. It's the summer of 1894 and, at least to begin with, the weather is nice (this won't last, of course, because summer in England is almost always a disappointment). But on with the story ...

CHAPTER 1

A Pioneer of the Skies

Everyone dreams about flying. Soaring above the clouds, banking your wings to make graceful curves through the air, swooping like a hawk from great heights. Jumping off the toolshed roof. Spending a week with a bandage round your head. Being told how lucky you were not to break your neck.

Everyone dreams about flying. Emmaline did.

Emmaline Cayley was a pioneering scientist. She had declared this when she turned eleven. She was a leader in the field of aeronautics, as she would tell anyone who would listen; at least, she would be one day. The girls she knew said that Emmaline was mad and that she probably still believed in fairies. Emmaline didn't care what other girls thought. She didn't care about dolls or new dresses or tea parties; *she* cared about aeronautics. She was an aviatrix. By her thirteenth birthday, Emmaline had decided that she was going to invent a flying machine. That was more than a year ago in Calcutta, India, where she had been brought up.

Now she was in England, waiting to go to boarding school.

Emmaline sat on a fallen tree, looking out over a valley. It was smooth grassland with no rocks, no trees or tangly bushes and no patches of bog to get sucked into. Emmaline considered it a perfect place for an experiment with flight. What she actually thought was, "This would be a fine place to try out a flying machine — if I had one — and could get somebody (but not me) to sit in it and see what happened when it left the ground."

The truth is that Emmaline was afraid of flying. She didn't admit this to herself, however. She told herself that if she were to plummet to her doom, then all her experimental knowledge as a pioneer in aeronautics would die with her. Emmaline thought this would be a tragedy indeed.

A pilot. She needed a pilot.

Emmaline's great-great-uncle, Sir George Cayley, had tried inventing flying machines long ago. As a boy he'd made model gliders, studied birds' wings and conducted strange experiments with wind tunnels. But he hadn't built an actual, full-sized flying machine until 1849, when he was much older. He had ordered a boy to sit in the machine. Sir George was seventy-six at the time, so nobody felt he was letting anyone down by not flying it himself (when you are ancient, you can get away with a lot). The contraption worked as Sir George had hoped, sailing through the air a hundred yards or thereabouts, and nobody was injured.

A few years later, Cayley tried again with a bigger, better craft. This time, Sir George "volunteered" his coachman, a light, skinny man (just the type he needed), to fly the glider. A team of big, brawny farmhands from Cayley's estate hauled it up a hill above a valley known as Brompton Dale. The machine was a marvel. The lads pushed, and it rose in the air, soared two hundred yards and landed in a meadow with a splintering, sickening crash. The coachman, John Appleby, tottered from the wreckage, limped back up the hill and resigned on the spot.

"Sir George, I wish to give notice. I was hired to drive, not to fly!"

Emmaline knew there was a simple moral to the story. Get somebody else to sit in the pilot's seat.

But where to find him?

Emmaline's daydreams were interrupted by a voice from behind her.

"Come in for tea, dear!" called Aunt Lucy. "There's some excellent nettle jam. Not really pleasant to taste, but full of nutrition."

Lucy Butterworth's notion of food was, frankly, appalling. She read journals with strange, "scientific" articles about healthy eating. She gathered what might be vegetables (or weeds) from her overgrown garden, from hedgerows and pastures and woods, and from roadside ditches. She collected slugs and worms and woodlice, too. Then she cooked them. Emmaline hoped that there would be no slugs in the cakes her aunt had baked today.

Emmaline rose from her log and walked to the gate. Aunt Lucy's smiling face peered over the wall. She was extremely short for a grown woman, though she made up for that with a waist measurement that was greater than her height. Unkind people in the village of Lower Owlthwaite, where Aunt Lucy lived, muttered to one another, asking how a woman who ate weeds and twigs could be so round. Those same unkind people would use words like "gangly" and "lanky" to describe Emmaline, when they knew her. (They didn't, yet, because Emmaline had only been staying with her aunt for three weeks.)

"Nice afternoon, dear?"

"Yes, Aunt Lucy," replied Emmaline. "I am trying to work out how to fly across the valley."

Most aunts would comment on this sort of statement. Possibly to say that it was ridiculous or impossible or life-threateningly dangerous. Lucy Butterworth wasn't one of those aunts.

"That's very nice, dear. Do you like rhubarb, centipede and dandelion crumble?" she asked.

They entered the house, a rambling old building that seemed to have grown in sections from a stone cottage. It was, indeed, a very higgledy-piggledy sort of house, with extra bits built on here and there over hundreds of years. People in the village called it "Mad Mrs. Butterworth's house" after Aunt Lucy. The mad lady with the odd food and the strange manners.

For some reason the house had two kitchens. Perhaps whoever had owned it in the first place had disliked the original and just built a new kitchen without removing the old one. Or perhaps there were relatives who disliked living

together so much that they couldn't bear to eat food from the same place. Aunt Lucy liked to say, "I never know where my next meal's coming from!" Emmaline laughed every time.

They went through the scullery, past the pantry, around one of the kitchens, up a flight of stairs, down another, round a corner and down a hall to the dining room.

Lal Singh had the table spread out like a banquet. He always did. No matter what the food itself might look like or taste like, Lal Singh was the perfect butler. He wore a long red tunic, a yellow turban and an air of polished perfection. Even his gleaming black beard seemed to be polished. Most houses didn't have butlers, especially crumbling old piles like Aunt Lucy's. Most butlers were dignified, quiet men in black clothes. Lal Singh was quiet and dignified, to be sure, but Emmaline understood that the tall Sikh was more than a servant. He wore the uniform of a regiment in the Queen's Indian Army. Uncle Cedric had been Lal Singh's commander, and now Lal Singh served his widow, Aunt Lucy.

"Lal Singh," began Emmaline as she nibbled at the edges of her watercress and earthworm sandwich, "do you know anything about flying?"

"No, miss, I do not."

"I bet he does," thought Emmaline. She believed that Lal Singh preferred not to reveal everything he knew.

She knew that Lal Singh did not eat Aunt Lucy's hideous food. She'd heard him tell her that his religion forbade him to eat the food made by an unbeliever. That was when Aunt Lucy had made him a special earwig curry as a surprise.

"I'm thinking of building a flying machine," said Emmaline. "Something that could carry a person through the sky. My great-great-uncle George built several, years ago. He made gliders, like kites really, with wings and room for a pilot. I want to make one that can go wherever I want. One day I'll make one with an engine of some kind."

"You mean like a railway locomotive, miss?" Lal Singh

spoke excellent English for a man who must have learned it as a grown-up. It was not the ordinary, dull language that Emmaline had learned. It was the English of India, with its different ways of pronouncing things, and a kind of lilt to how one said it. Lal Singh had a sort of twinkle in his voice, which Emmaline liked very much. It was good to hear again, so far from Calcutta and the life she had left behind.

"Well, perhaps," replied Emmaline. "But something much smaller. If it was as heavy as a railway engine, it would never be able to stay in the air. You'd need wings the size of a football pitch, and balloons to lift it and —"

Emmaline wasn't sure what you'd need. She'd read books and articles and Sir George's volumes on the science of aeronautics. But they were hard to follow, full of tiny diagrams and odd words that she didn't really understand. And, since he had died thirty-seven years ago, she couldn't ask him.

So, Emmaline still didn't have a pilot. And she didn't have anything for him to pilot in.

CHAPTER 2

Rubberbones

Actually, Emmaline did have a pilot. She just didn't know it yet. *He* didn't know it yet. His name was Robert Burns and he lived in Lower Owlthwaite with his grandmother. He had been named after the Scottish poet because, as his father had said, he was going to be called Burns anyway, so he might as well be named after the famous one.

This Robert Burns wasn't a poet. And he wasn't from Scotland. If anyone called him a "muckle wee bairn" or some such piece of Scottishness, he would have probably responded by simply staring at them. He was a local lad, a Yorkshire lad. His father had run away from home to seek his fortune. (This is a good thing to do when you are young and independent; it's not so good when you are thirty-four and have a wife and five children, like Mr. Burns.) Robert's mother had gone to London to stay with family, taking his brother and sisters; he'd stayed with his gran in Lower Owlthwaite to work. There wasn't much money coming in, so he had to help out. He had left school when he was ten, and now he made pennies doing odd jobs, sometimes for odd people. He would clean out gutters or put loose slates back on roofs. He would even climb inside chimneys to sweep them clean; he was small, and nobody had told him it was incredibly dangerous. He fell off things and out of things and down things. He never got hurt. He got a new name.

"Rubberbones." That's what the village children called him. It was an easy change from "Robert Burns," and it seemed to fit. When the local lads played their own strange kind of football in a farmer's field, Rubberbones was never bruised, scuffed, scragged or bent. Village football wasn't a gentleman's sport. It involved kicking or carrying or throwing a ball from one end of a field to the other in any way humanly possible. It was a rough, tussling event that involved dozens of boys and men and went on for hours until it got too dark to see. Rain didn't stop it. Blood didn't stop it. The last thing that had disrupted the game was the plague, five hundred years ago (*that* cut down on the numbers coming out every week). No weapons were allowed, and not too much in the way of biting. And although young Robert was only twelve, and small for his age, he was a hero in the village. He was very quick and nimble and — since he never got hurt — he was very brave.

His gran called him "Rab." She really *was* Scottish.

One day he came to do odd jobs at Aunt Lucy's house. Cleaning out the gutters, checking for loose tiles and generally clambering about on the roof.

Emmaline sat contemplating her future. Her mother and father were still in India, where Mr. Cayley held an important job in the government. This was during the time when the British ruled India. In the summer, the Cayleys lived in Simla, high in the Himalayas. Emmaline had thought it a wonderland of towering peaks and fresh air. The rest of the year, they had lived in Calcutta, which Emmaline knew as a city of interesting people, food and colors. Her parents thought it was a hot, sticky place full of disease and poverty and not suitable for a nice English child to grow up in. Mainly, it was Emmaline's mother who thought this. Mr. Cayley was always off in some distant place, doing something vital for "the Viceroy," the most important person in India. Even when her father was home, he had no time for her at all. He spent hours poring over books and reports. Her mother hated India, but Emmaline loved it. However, Mrs. Cayley wanted Emmaline to go to a proper girls' school and learn manners and etiquette and music and drawing and French. A school in England.

So, in a few weeks, Emmaline was going to a boarding school for girls. A good one, everyone had said, recommended by someone her mother knew — a sour widow called Mrs. Bloodless whose husband had been someone important. She held a "position of influence" among the British ladies, which meant she was immensely bossy and snobbish and liked to be as rude as she could. If Mrs. Bloodless had an opinion, however mean and unpleasant, she would express it. Nobody ever argued with her. She said that girls shouldn't be allowed to run wild and that they needed a dose of strict discipline. Take Emmaline Cayley, for example; she certainly needed a suitable education, according to the widow. She should be learning the proper subjects for young ladies, "not wasting her time dreaming of flying machines." Emmaline had overheard Mrs. Bloodless say exactly that. A month later it was all arranged, and Emmaline's destiny was determined.

Emmaline was sitting on a bench under the eaves of Aunt Lucy's house, lost in thought, when a small boy came crashing down off the roof. He landed just inches from her, smashing into an ornamental birdbath. Tumbling among fallen slates, the boy lay on the flagstones, legs pointed upward. The water from the shattered birdbath was gurgling down, emptying onto his hair. It looked like the first bath he'd had in a good while.

"Ey-oop, miss," he said. "Er, sorry about that. Is the missus about?" He gestured all around him. "I had a bit of an accident."

Aunt Lucy appeared at the open window. The crash must have been loud enough to hear in the kitchen. Both kitchens. "I've got some wonderful ointment made from stinging nettles!" she announced. She came out with a huge box of bandages to tend to the boy's injuries. Aunt Lucy looked him over, but the boy didn't seem to have a single bruise.

"Well, well!" she said. "Well!" She wrapped his head up anyway, and one of his ankles.

"I'll pay for the damage, missus!" said the lad.

"Nonsense!" insisted Aunt Lucy. "You fell off *my* roof onto *my* birdbath! I should be paying you. It was a revolting birdbath and has been here far too long. You've done me a favor!" She shunted him into the kitchen, patting him to make sure there really weren't any dangerous wounds she had missed.

"I never get 'urt, missus. I'm indestruckable. I am, honest," he said.

"You're a lucky lad. It's a miracle. Have a sandwich!" Aunt Lucy replied, thrusting a watercress-and-earthworm sandwich at him. There were still plenty of leftovers from the day before.

Emmaline, standing behind Aunt Lucy, shook her head violently at the boy. Falling twenty feet onto ornamental thingummybobs was one thing, but having to eat Aunt Lucy's sandwiches was quite another.

But the boy gobbled down the first sandwich and reached for a second.

Emmaline was amazed. Horrified as well, but mostly amazed. She gawped at the boy. It wasn't ladylike to gawp, but there you have it. Not being ladylike was one of the many things her mother had said that she must change.

"What's your name, then?" asked Emmaline.

"My real name is Robert Burns, but everyone calls me Rubberbones. Except for my gran. She calls me Rab."

However, having his mouth full of the appalling sandwich, and not having been told never to talk with his mouth full, what he actually said was, "MreenebiRobbberberrberevrncor meeRubberberrsepmeegrancorrmeeRab."

Emmaline understood perfectly.

"Good morning, Rab," she said, "or Rubberbones."

"The boy who falls out of the sky. The boy who doesn't get hurt. The boy who will eat watercress-and-earthworm sandwiches. The ideal person for the job," she thought to herself.

One problem solved, then.

CHAPTER 3

A Contraption

Emmaline knew that her uncle Cedric had fallen fatally from a camel and left Aunt Lucy with a tumbledown house, enough money to do what she liked and the chance to become an eccentric old lady. Encouraging her niece to build a flying machine was exactly the sort of thing she loved to do.

"I should like to start work on my flying machine," declared Emmaline after Rab had gone home. She was helping her aunt arrange jars of jellied snails along the top of a piano in the parlor. "May I have an advance on my pocket money, Aunt Lucy? I need to buy tools, wood, fabric, glue, screws and some other things."

Emmaline had made up a seven-page list of all those other things.

"Why yes, of course, dear," replied her aunt. "Will you be using the old stable as a workshop?"

"Yes, and, er, that boy," said Emmaline.

"Boy, dear?"

"Um, yes, the one who nearly fell on me," Emmaline replied.

"Nice boy. Good eater. Twelve sandwiches! Rubbery lad — jolly close to unbreakable, they say."

"Can we ask him to be the pilot?" Emmaline wondered. "Since he's unbreakable."

"Splendid idea! I'll mention it to his grandmother. I can't imagine she'd object," said Aunt Lucy. She began to play a jaunty melody on the piano to celebrate this great new plan, and all the jars wobbled, and the jellied snails spun around.

——◇◆◇——

Rubberbones's grandmother was happy to have him work for Mad Mrs. Butterworth. The major's widow had no idea about wages and had offered Rab twice what anybody in Lower Owlthwaite would pay. To Rab, "It were champion!" It wasn't just the money, which he'd send to his mother; it was the adventure, the discovery, the jumping off roofs.

The next step was buying supplies. It was easy to purchase wood from the timber merchant and heavy cotton canvas from Mrs. Wimberley's shop in the High Street. Mr. Peacock, the village ironmonger, provided tools, screws, nails and the like. Aunt Lucy ordered brass widgets and gutta-percha (which sounded an awful lot like a fish, but wasn't one) from places in London and Sheffield; Emmaline had looked up the addresses in her dog-eared copy of *Inventor's Monthly Reader, incorporating Scientific Presbyterian Digest* for April of 1891.

What was difficult was that Emmaline had no actual idea of how to build a flying machine. She had no step-by-step instructions to go by, so she'd have to make it up as she went along. She *did* have the diagrams drawn by her great-great ancestor, Sir George, so she pored over these. And before long, with the help of Rubberbones and Lal Singh, she had built the framework of wood struts, brass braces and thingummies of leather and whalebone and the mysterious gutta-percha.

Aunt Lucy sewed lengths of canvas cloth to cover the frames. They looked at Sir George's plans from 1849 and 1853. Then they looked at what they had made so far. The contraption didn't seem anything like the plans. Had they built a clotheshorse that hoped to be a tent? An imitation chicken? They couldn't really believe that it was a flying machine.

But Rubberbones could.

"Let's give it a go, then!" he said.

This was the time that sensible, responsible grown-ups would smile and shake their heads at the foolishness of children. Aunt Lucy smiled. Lal Singh smiled. Then they all carried the flying machine up onto the roof. Rubberbones was belted into a deck chair facing forward, among the flaps and wings and bits of basketwork. He was grinning like a chimpanzee.

"Are you sure you are all right with this?" asked Emmaline. "It does seem awfully dangerous."

But as she said it, Rubberbones raised both hands and shouted something like "Wheeeee!!!!" The contraption lurched forward. It slid down the sloping tiles toward the valley, the beautiful, grassy valley without bushes or rocks, tangles or marshes. The valley just beyond Aunt Lucy's overgrown garden with its bushes and trees and —

"Oh," called Rab in a small voice. "I think I'm stuck in this tree."

Indeed, he *was* stuck in a tree. And he was upside down, too. But at least he wasn't broken, which was not true of the flying machine. The Cayley Gliding Craft, Mark I, which had looked like a tent from one angle, a chicken from another and a clotheshorse from a third, now looked like —

Bits of broken wood strewn across a garden.

Some canvas sheets, torn up into shreds.

A deck chair in a tree.

A small (but lively) boy, also in the tree.

"Jolly good start!" cried Aunt Lucy. "I'll make some brussels sprout punch for everyone. It's very refreshing."

But it wasn't a good start as far as Emmaline was concerned. The machine had smashed up, and the pilot was lucky to be in one piece, no matter what he said about being unbreakable.

Emmaline had thought she had everything she needed: a detailed set of plans for a flying machine, an indestructible boy who had thoroughly enjoyed crashing into a tree and an eccentric aunt who would pay for any madcap scheme her niece could come up with. Still, it wasn't enough.

———

It was the third week of July, ten days after the Trial Flight, as Emmaline chose to call it. She was trying to pretend it wasn't a disaster. Lal Singh had measured the distance between the top of the roof and the beech tree that the glider had crashed into. It was nineteen feet and seven inches. Still, Rubberbones saw it as an improvement on his first effort.

"I missed that birdbath completely this time, Miss Em," he declared cheerfully.

Emmaline had told him to call her that, and he seemed to like it. She called him "Robert" when she was educating him into the mysteries of science and "Rab" at other times. They were looking at a book, *Mad Birdmen through the Ages*. Emmaline explained some of the stories in it.

"It all started with Daedalus and Icarus," she said.

"You what? What's them?" demanded the boy.

"Daedalus and Icarus. It's an old story. A Greek myth. Daedalus was an inventor in ancient times. The king imprisoned him and his son, Icarus, in a tower. Daedalus made wings out of feathers and wax —"

"Ey-oop," said Rubberbones. (Emmaline didn't know what that meant, but it seemed to show interest.) "They just had feathers and wax lying about, then? In prison?"

"I suppose they must have," she answered. "They had to make their own entertainment in those days. Anyway, they flew out to freedom, but Icarus flew too close to the sun. The wax in his wings melted, and he fell to his death."

Rubberbones thought about it. "I'll 'ave to remember that. I'll try not to get too close to the sun." He smiled, as if that was agreed.

Emmaline read to him about the various inventions that aimed to see a man (always a man, it seemed) fly. Four hundred years before, Leonardo da Vinci, the artist who had painted the famous *Mona Lisa*, had made sketches of winged men and odd machines. Nobody knew if he'd ever tried to make one. Since his time, there had been many efforts by people who thought that just by impersonating a bird, they could fly. Only the lucky ones survived. Most of them broke various bones. The Italian traveler Marco Polo reported that in China, prisoners were tied to huge kites and flown on windy days. They didn't seem to enjoy it.

Emmaline noticed that although Rubberbones didn't read very well, he showed a real interest in the details of the drawings. Not just the ones that showed desperate birdmen flapping wildly before smashing into the ground (people would always enjoy those). No, Rubberbones looked carefully at the complicated plans for flying machines, the ones with exact measurements. Still, he did like the illustration of a Chinese criminal lashed to a huge kite as a punishment. But then, who wouldn't?

————

Two days later Emmaline caught sight of her new assistant from her bedroom window. Rubberbones was right outside. He was strapped to a very large kite with the kind of tape you might use for parcels. One end of the string was wrapped around the garden bench. This was fortunate, as the kite itself was not really flying so much as fighting fierce gusts of wind. The blast was battering the sail-like kite, knocking it this way and that. All the time, Rubberbones was grinning from ear to ear. His wrists were tied in place, so he couldn't move. All he could do was flap about with the kite, which surely could not stand up to the powerful winds for much longer.

Emmaline flung open her window. The gale was blowing ferociously.

"Rab! What the — how did you —?"

She could barely hear her own voice. She couldn't hear his at all. But she could hear a voice from behind her. It was Aunt Lucy.

"What a nice young man he is, that Robert. I've been watching him for twenty minutes. We should probably go and rescue him now."

With Lal Singh's help, Emmaline and Aunt Lucy were able to haul down the kite. It was torn and beginning to rip apart. The boy attached to it was a bit torn up himself. He had lost some buttons from his shirt, and his hair stuck out in all directions. He seemed deliriously happy.

"That were champion, that were!" he announced.

As they took Rubberbones into the house (his teeth were chattering, but he kept smiling like the Cheshire Cat in *Alice's Adventures in Wonderland*), Emmaline realized something. She had spent ages reading about flying. Thinking about flying. Talking about flying. And then along came this boy who never read at all, who had never thought about flying until a few weeks ago, and he simply went out and flew.

───────

Lal Singh had brought the remains of Rubberbones's kite into the old stable. There was more to it than Emmaline would have guessed. It was, at first sight, a typical child's kite — brown paper, string, a frame of wooden crosspieces — although much larger than usual. But there were some differences.

"What's this bit here?" she asked, pointing at a piece of bent wood.

"Oh, that's for stability," explained Rubberbones. "Keeps you from turning upside down-like. You can see the same thing in your great-great-uncle's drawings. And this bit, wi' a curve on top but flat underneath, that's copied off him too." He held up the roughly carved plank. "I used me gran's kitchen knife to cut it. It's the shape of a bird's wing. Sir George called it an *aerofoil*."

Stability? Aerofoil? These were scientific terms that Emmaline had seen in Sir George's instructions. She wasn't really sure she understood them herself. Now, suddenly, Rab was speaking as if they were ordinary, everyday things. She realized that he was explaining "lift" and "drag."

"Would you say that again, Robert?" asked Emmaline.

"Lift is what gets under you and takes you up in the air. Like an umbrella on a windy day. Drag is what makes you go backward on a windy day when you're trying to walk forward but the gusts are too strong."

Emmaline nodded. The books she had read had never explained it so easily.

"So, when you fly, Miss Em, you want lots of the one — lift — and not much of t'other — drag."

Later, when Rubberbones had gone home, Emmaline asked her aunt about watching the boy lashed to a kite in the gale.

"Why didn't you try to stop him, Aunt Lucy?"

Her aunt considered the question.

"Robert was, in some way, born to fly. Robert flies because he doesn't know that he can't. I certainly won't tell him that he can't fly."

Emmaline felt more hopeful than she'd ever felt before. Between her and this strange boy, they would make a flying machine. Not a kite or a crashing contraption but something that would really take to the air and fly.

Chapter 4

Another Contraption

The new flying machine was different from the first one. It was made of the same things — wood and canvas, brass bits and screws, most of which had come from the wreck of the first flyer. What was different this time was that Emmaline and Rubberbones worked together with a real plan. The first machine had been a contraption based on looking at Sir George's drawings from long ago but not really understanding what they meant.

Emmaline and Rubberbones worked hour by hour, following the old plans carefully. This time they weren't just going to drag the machine up on the roof and hope that it could clear the trees in the garden. They had thought of a better place, with a tall tower overlooking open grass. St. Cuthbert's Church, Lower Owlthwaite. But it would have to be arranged. It might not be allowed.

Aunt Lucy took Emmaline to talk to the vicar.

The vicar was the sort of kindly old fellow who seems to be surprised at everything. And, in Emmaline's case, he had reason to be. People usually came to the vicar to ask about getting married at the church or having their children baptized. They came to ask him if he could please stop his delinquent dog, Stanley, from digging in their flowerbeds. What people did not ask the vicar was whether they could take advantage of the church's handsome bell tower to launch a gliding machine.

But Emmaline did, with some prompting from her aunt.

"Please, Reverend, can we use the church tower to launch a flying machine — sort of a big kite — with my friend Rab — that's Robert Burns — strapped inside, and we won't be any trouble, honestly?"

It wasn't a very good request. She was nervous about asking.

Emmaline liked the vicar, and she hoped he felt the same about her. Aunt Lucy had brought her to church every

Sunday since she had come to the village. Emmaline didn't sleep during the sermons or cough during the prayers. Vicars notice things like that.

Emmaline knew that there were many reasons why the vicar should have said that he'd have to discuss it with the parish council, or the bishop, or the verger, or the Ladies' Afternoon Flower-Arranging Society. Aunt Lucy had told Emmaline that there were all sorts of people who told the vicar what to do.

But, frankly, the vicar was sick of all of them. Aunt Lucy had told Emmaline that he'd done exactly as they'd instructed him for thirty years. He was retiring next month. Emmaline hoped he'd show the busybodies what he thought of them.

"Yes! By all means!" the vicar responded to Emmaline's request. "An excellent plan! More tea, dear ladies?"

The vicar was going to read cowboy stories and carve wooden elephants, take long walks with Stanley — a wild, untrained small dog of boundless enthusiasm for life and petty destruction — and never listen to any of those busybodies ever again. And he'd start by allowing experimental aeronauts to fly off the bell tower, no matter what anyone else thought or said.

———

Now it was just a question of the right day.

First of all, it was no good trying to fly on a rainy day. Emmaline didn't want her first successful venture into the world of aviation to be marred by rain. That would be depressing.

Second, she didn't want to get the machine wet, because wet cloth becomes heavy. The canvas wings and sails had to be light to ride the gusts of wind coming up over the valley.

But mainly, Emmaline simply wanted a nice day. As anyone would.

The winds would have to be fresh, but not too strong —

a nice breeze from the west that would lift the flyer gently and let the machine glide across the open fields to land in a smooth meadow a few hundred yards away. Too much wind might send the glider swirling to destruction below, or hurl it high into the heavens, or simply carry the thing miles and miles, far out to sea.

And no wind at all would be useless.

"I think Wednesday will be perfect, dear," announced Aunt Lucy out of the blue.

Tuesday's post brought a letter from India and another from St. Grimelda's School for Young Ladies. Emmaline opened the one from her mother first.

> *Dearest, darling Emmaline,*
>
> *Simla is simply gorgeous this year. So much nicer than horrid, horrid Calcutta. Do you remember Colonel and Mrs. Twembly-Watchit, whom we had over for croquet last year? Well, they have a simply darling little . . .*

And it went on like this for page after page.

Then it took what Emmaline could only see as a nasty turn for the worse:

> *You are to begin as a pupil at St. Grimelda's on the first of September. Whilst I have no doubt that it will seem strange to you, I am sure you will get used to it. It has a fine reputation as one of England's oldest and strictest schools for girls. Mrs. Bloodless highly recommends it. Her sister was having terrible problems with a willful daughter who engaged in idle chatter, dancing and unnecessary kindness to servants. After five years at St. Grimelda's, the girl was perfectly well*

behaved and, in fact, never left her bedroom again.
(Tragically, she died when she accidentally swallowed
poison three days in a row.) The headmistress writes
that they pride themselves on firm discipline and
not fussing over idle fripperies that spoil young girls so.
Since you've never liked fripperies, I am sure you'll like
it well enough . . .

Emmaline knew the word "frippery" — it usually meant
the kind of silly, lacy, pointlessness of foolish females quite
unlike herself, who knew nothing of science and invention.
But what did it mean to St. Grimelda's?
The letter finished with another worrying paragraph.

Your father has forwarded sufficient funds for your
uniform and sundry needs directly to the school. As
you know, I have always considered your aunt Lucy
(dear Lucy, a darling, sweet creature!) to be somewhat
flighty in her moods. Please do not attempt to
persuade her to make alternative arrangements for
your education, as we are determined that St.
Grimelda's is the perfect place to mold your character
and instill discipline in your wayward attitudes.
Much love and kisses! Your father sends his regards,
Mumsie

The letter from St. Grimelda's was short and strict.
Beneath a printed coat of arms, featuring a black tower and
a large padlock, it began:

Miss Cayley,

You are to report shortly to this school for educational
purposes. Please do not even consider attempting to
avoid this necessity. The arrangements are firm and
will not be altered.

Emmaline thought this might be the most threatening letter of welcome ever sent. It continued with a list of everything a new girl would need, which seemed to be a lot of uniform clothing in the school colors (black, dark gray and charcoal) with special emphasis on hygienic woolen underwear (also in the school colors). There was a longer list of things that the new arrival was not allowed to bring. These included anything that might be remotely interesting or enjoyable.

Books, dolls, toys and other childish items are strictly forbidden. No food may be brought in. Non-uniform clothing will be confiscated.

She was allowed one small photograph: *of family members, not smiling.* It was signed *Malvolia Wackett, Headmistress.* Emmaline felt a shiver run through her.

Wednesday was, as Aunt Lucy had predicted, perfect. Well, almost. The sun was shining, the breeze was brisk and businesslike. The vicar had allowed Emmaline to store the flyer inside the bell tower for the maiden flight of the flying machine. This meant that for days the church bell could not be rung, which infuriated Mr. Peel, the bell ringer. The vicar had been annoyed with Mr. Peel for the past thirty years, so this worked out perfectly, as far as he was concerned.

The only thing wrong with Wednesday was that it was the day of the annual football match between Lower Owlthwaite and the village two miles up the valley, known as Upper Owlthwaite. The two Owlthwaites had been bitter rivals since the time of the Vikings, and the match was always, in the words of the local paper, "keenly contested." Hundreds of people would be there. Spectators came from miles around. Everybody knew about the match. Everyone except eccentric old ladies like Aunt Lucy.

The teams were supposed to consist of twenty-seven men,

youths or boys from each village. No girls were allowed because they had proven far too savage in the past. Among the twenty-seven men of Lower Owlthwaite was Rubberbones. The team saw him as both an ace player and a sort of mascot. He had been chosen by the village committee, which had planned the team strategy over pints of beer at the Stick and Ferret. It was a tremendous honor.

The match was due to start at ten.

It should have been obvious that Rubberbones could not play football and pilot the flying machine on the same day. He'd have to choose between them. But he didn't. He could have mentioned the football match to Emmaline or her aunt, and they could have waited for another fine day to come along. The summer had been warm and sunny for the first month, before the rain and wind, fog and hail that mark July in England had set in. There must be at least one more fine, breezy day, surely?

Rubberbones wasn't so certain. So he made a plan. A brilliant plan, he believed. He could pilot the flyer off the church tower, take a quick glide over the village meadow to see what was going on, land the machine just over the brow of the hill and run back to score a hatful of goals for Lower Owlthwaite. Maybe he'd even have time for a bacon sandwich. He'd be a hero twice over. It was the perfect solution.

So Rubberbones never said a word to Emmaline about the football match. And Emmaline, being new in the village, didn't know anything about the tradition.

Rubberbones was ready to fly at dawn. He wore a padded costume made by Aunt Lucy. Actually, it was trousers and an old sweater belonging to her late husband, stuffed with all sorts of rags and far too large for Rubberbones. She'd found a sort of helmet, like something out of the days of chivalry (if knights of old liked red wooly things) and a pair of goggles. Emmaline said he looked gallant, which wasn't really true. She inspected him before they climbed up the bell tower. "Good work, Rab!" she said.

The vicar was already atop the tower. He had made a starter's flag from a piece of red flannel and a stick. Nobody had seen the old chap quite so excited since the time Mrs. Scoggs brought her elderberry wine (which had turned to brandy) to the village festival and given it out in mugfuls to everyone.

The plan was to launch the flyer from a wooden ramp that ran down the tower roof. It looked like a children's slide. Until two days ago, it *had* been a children's slide. Lal Singh had found it, and the vicar had taken it up to the tower and nailed it in position. After so many years at St. Cuthbert's, always doing the right thing and following the rules, the vicar was thrilled to behave like a schoolboy.

If the plan had gone off at dawn, everything would have been fine. Rubberbones would have piloted the flyer, had breakfast and gone to play in the annual football match. But Aunt Lucy and Lal Singh (for reasons involving the need to pick nice, fresh dandelions in a field six miles away) arrived at nine-thirty. "Ever so sorry! Lost track of the time! Marvelous dandelions!" trilled Aunt Lucy. That changed things completely.

At last, Aunt Lucy and Lal Singh were in position in the meadow, ready for the flyer's landing. They had spread out a very large red blanket so that Rubberbones would have something to aim for. The distance was about four hundred yards, although there was no reason to worry if Rubberbones fell short. At least, there would be no reason to worry as long as there was nobody on the village green.

Today there were hundreds of people gathering on the village green.

Rubberbones looked out from the tower. He could see the swarming crowds of spectators, the man selling hot sausages and pies and the ladies who brought homemade cakes and tea. The Stick and Ferret was selling ale to the crowds. He could see the teams warming up, one side in blue shirts, the other in white. There was a great deal of good-natured pushing and shoving, with a bit of wrestling, gouging and poking on the side.

The match began with a whistle. A man in a flat red cap placed the ball on the ground, and immediately a massive brawl erupted. It was hard to tell the players from the spectators; lots of onlookers had jumped into the fray. This meant that rather than having twenty-seven men on each team, the villages each had somewhere between fifty and a hundred players. Some were useful, others just got in the way.

"Good Lord, Robert!" exclaimed Emmaline. "Did you know about this?"

"Er, no, miss." Rubberbones blushed furiously. Emmaline had to know he was lying.

"But it'll be all right, Miss Em."

Emmaline hoped it would. It was a big day for her plans, and she desperately wished that the flyer would soar. She hadn't expected a huge crowd to come and see it.

She certainly hadn't expected a huge crowd to come for something else completely different.

Just then the vicar, who had been testing the wind with a child's hand-held toy windmill, called out, "Time to fly, young man!" His dog, Stanley, barked in agreement and seized the toy windmill in his mouth. The vicar waved the starter's flag.

Across the field, Aunt Lucy waved her own flag in reply.

Rubberbones still thought it would be all right. No, it'd be champion. He'd be the first player to arrive in a flying machine. He just hoped he wouldn't miss more than a few minutes of the match.

The vicar, waving his flag about like a small boy, cried out, "Tallyho! Soar like a bird, young fellow!"

Then he and Emmaline pushed the flyer off the ramp. Stanley barked once again, approvingly.

CHAPTER 5

Which Starts Well Enough

The flying machine slid down the ramp, picking up speed as it went. Rubberbones was hunched, motionless. He dared not breathe. The craft nosed beyond the edge of the tower roof, and for a moment Emmaline thought the machine was going to tip over and plunge. But the wind caught under the wings, bearing the glider upward. The nose was angled toward the horizon, and air currents pushed the machine onward, making it soar over the village green.

Below, the crowd stood and stared. Not all at once, but one by one the spectators fell silent. Some pointed upward. The players at the edge of the scrimmage stopped pushing their neighbors and looked up in wonder.

The glider flew straight and true. The craft ghosted over the meadow toward the soft, cushiony grass in front of Aunt Lucy and Lal Singh. Rab thought it was the best flying machine ever made.

The vicar and Emmaline waved madly, he with the flag, she with a handkerchief. Across the field Aunt Lucy was waving her own flag, and Lal Singh was smiling.

Rubberbones had planned on waving, but he was entranced by the view. So many people. So small, at first, then growing larger as the flyer descended. He was over the football pitch now. He flew over the barrow of the man selling sausages and passed right above the cake ladies. Rab landed with a soft thud, about fifty feet short of the red blanket. The glider had no wheels to land on, but the base had a smooth runner crafted by Lal Singh to slide across the grass.

Emmaline thought it was perfect. The vicar cheered like a lunatic.

Rubberbones was ready to play. It'd just take him a minute to get out.

If nothing else had happened, it would have been "champion," as he always said. He'd have climbed out, run over to the meadow and hurled himself into the fray.

But that wasn't what happened at all.

The ball hit him hard on the back of the head, as someone shouted, "Rubberbones! Yer late! Run wi' t'ball, lad! Dribble!"

The players all chased after it.

Lal Singh would have been there first, but he waited for Aunt Lucy, and Aunt Lucy had short legs. A mob, in white and blue, burst through the cake tables, over the sausage barrow, on toward the flying machine. Exactly where the ball was, nobody knew. Rubberbones sat in the little seat of the contraption, looking stunned and rubbing his head. He was not dribbling or running with the ball, as his teammate had hoped. He was just sitting there, confused. Possibly concussed.

The mob surged over the flying machine. Emmaline looked on in horror as dozens of players clambered over the flyer. She saw them stamping and tearing, rending and breaking. She saw Lal Singh picking up large men, one in each hand, and tossing them aside. Aunt Lucy was flailing away with her flag at the players. "Oh, biff them!" shouted the vicar. "*I* would!"

Emmaline ran down from the tower, through the church door and across the village green. "I hope I'm not too late to do anything!" she said to herself.

But she was.

By the time Emmaline got there, the machine was reduced to tatters and splinters. The players had gone, chasing the ball up the field and knocking over the sausage

barrow once again. Lal Singh had picked up the biggest
piece of wood left on the ground. It was eighteen inches
long, and you couldn't tell what it had been part of.

Rubberbones was nowhere to be seen.

Aunt Lucy saw the expression on Emmaline's face.

"Oh well, dear," she said, patting the girl on the shoulder.
"These things happen. I thought it went rather well, until
the very end."

CHAPTER 6

The Gypsies

Rubberbones didn't come back. At first everyone simply assumed that he had joined in the football match. Emmaline soon found out that far from not knowing anything about it, Robert Burns was the star player for Lower Owlthwaite. Yet he had never mentioned that this Wednesday was the most important day of the year to most of the village, an event that everyone — except Emmaline, her aunt and, apparently, the vicar — had known about for months. If Lal Singh had known, he'd kept quiet about it.

Emmaline wondered if Rubberbones had decided to give up his big day because of her? Had nobody even asked if there was anything else he had to do? Ever? Did she treat him as if he was a kind of servant, doing dangerous things that she didn't much fancy doing for herself? Was he just like Sir George Cayley's coachman who, that day in 1853, had flown, crashed and resigned then and there? Emmaline suddenly felt very bad indeed.

The destruction of the flying machine wasn't important. It was just cloth and wood and brass bits and glue. She'd built two of them now. She could build another. It was Rab she was worried about.

Two days later, Aunt Lucy knocked on Emmaline's bedroom door.

"You must stop this moping about, dear. You can't stay

in here forever," said Aunt Lucy. She bustled in with a tray of hideous weevil biscuits and vile pondwater tea. Emmaline could recognize the smell.

She made a pathetic sort of groaning noise.

"Get up, girl! I think I know where that silly boy has gone off to." Aunt Lucy sounded businesslike.

Emmaline stuck her head out from under the covers. "You do?"

"Lal Singh took me down to see Mrs. Burns," explained Aunt Lucy. "I assumed that young Robert was just hiding there, as you are doing here. But his grandmother hasn't seen him. The village team lost the football match, and some of the men say that if Robert had been there instead of "wasting his time with contraptions," Lower Owlthwaite would have got the trophy for winning ten years in a row. Nine years of victory and then their best player jumps off the church tower, runs off and Upper Owlthwaite wins a surprise 41–40 victory."

Emmaline sat up in surprise. "How do you know this? Until Wednesday you'd never even heard about the football match."

"Well, I know now," said Aunt Lucy. "I asked a lot of people. In the pub. They seemed surprised. Apparently mad old ladies like myself don't usually go to the Stick and Ferret."

Emmaline thought that was probably true.

"Well, anyway, the point is that people were saying that Rubberbones cost the village the gold cup. Apparently, it was last won in 1709 by Upper Owlthwaite, and never yet by our team. So Robert ran away."

"Ran away!" Emmaline was horrified.

"Ran away to join a band of traveling Gypsies, dear," added Aunt Lucy.

Emmaline was open-mouthed in astonishment.

Aunt Lucy continued. "His grandmother says that he always talks about running away with the Gypsies. Every year they come and camp outside the village and leave around this time. Robert's fascinated by their way of life. Every year he says he's running off with them. This year he actually has. Lal Singh's going to find out where they've gone. Do you know, by the way, that Gypsies originally came from India? They call themselves Roma or Romany and . . ."

While her aunt twittered on about the history and traditions of the proud Romany people so foolishly disliked by many villagers, Emmaline put on her traveling clothes. She was going to find her friend and bring him back.

———

The brightly painted caravans were camped and the horses set free to graze. The Romany band was settled for the night, the fires were blazing and a violinist was practicing ancient melodies from a place and time far away. It was the music that brought a weary Yorkshire boy into the camp. "Please, sir," he said to the first person he met, a tall man with fierce mustachios and curly black hair, "I've run away from home. I want to join the Gypsies."

The man sighed as if this kind of thing happened all the time, which it did.

"You'd best see the *barossan*, the chief, then," he replied gruffly.

Rubberbones did not know it, but children ran away to join the Gypsies all the time. The Gypsies had decided ages ago that this was not a good thing. The last thing a Gypsy band needs is young outsiders eating their food, taking up space and generally not contributing in any useful way. What's worse is that *gorgios* had a belief that Gypsies wanted to abduct their children. Possibly to sell. Or to eat. So having runaways suddenly show up was not what a Gypsy would want at all.

The *barossan* was an old man of great wisdom, grace and kindness. He had long white hair, gold earrings and a handsome coat of velveteen. He was accustomed to *gorgio* children. He had long ago decided that if outsider younglings ran away to his camp, he'd at least feed them, keep them safe and send out word so that their families could come and take them home. There was a question that he always asked of children who wanted to travel with the band. "What can you do that a Gypsy cannot?"

Usually, they had no answer. But Rubberbones did.

"I never get 'urt an' you can bounce me on my head an' I don't break an' I used to be able to fly but now I can't so I run away instead."

All in a rush, just like that.

The chief had never heard such an answer.

"I'll prove it to you," said Rubberbones. "I'll just climb up on that caravan and jump off."

"To fly?" asked the old man. This made him nervous. Nobody wants a broken-necked runaway boy lying about the place when the family come looking. It's very hard to explain.

"Nawsirr," replied Rubberbones. "I told you I can't do that anymore. No, I'll just fall off. But I won't break. I'll bounce."

The chief was a wise man, which is how he had held the post for forty years.

"No need at all, son. You look like a boy who can bounce. Do you like rhubarb pie?"

Rubberbones did, of course, and immediately forgot about jumping off the caravan roof.

Later on, when Rab was asleep under a wagon, wrapped up in a borrowed blanket, the chief told his eldest son to find out whom this boy belonged to — and soon.

Emmaline and Lal Singh rode in the cart along the rutted, bumpy track. They were a long way off the main road, going uphill toward the high ridge of the Pennines, the long chain of peaks that formed the spine of northern England. Lal Singh knew where Rubberbones was. He'd met someone who'd met a Gypsy who was, it seemed, anxious to find the people who owned a bouncing boy.

"How did you find him so quickly, Lal Singh?" asked Emmaline.

The Sikh laughed. "It was quite simple, miss. The Gypsies are easy to track. So I followed through the places they had camped. Then I met a Romany coming from the other direction looking for me."

"But how did he know you?" asked Emmaline.

"Because I was looking for him."

Emmaline scratched her head in confusion.

She was still trying to understand when the cart came round a bend in the track. The hedges and trees opened out into a clearing. There were wagons of many shapes, painted in bold designs and vivid colors. Dark, handsome men wore silken scarves and silver earrings. Dark, beautiful women in flowing gowns and flashing smiles danced. Guitars and violins played haunting, sinuous music far different from the folk music of England. And a freckled boy stood just beyond the campfire, wearing a sign that proclaimed, "THE INDIA-RUBBER BOY! SEE HIM BOUNCE!"

Though, in truth, it said "BONCE" and "INDEA" because the India-rubber boy couldn't spell very well.

They had found him. Now to take him home.

Rubberbones appeared forlorn. He had been shouting for people to hit him, strike him with sticks, throw him up in the air, whatever they liked. But none of the Gypsies wanted to take full advantage of his bouncing abilities.

"Hello, Rab," said Emmaline. "How are you today?"

This was the approach she'd decided on beforehand. Not, "We've come to take you home," or, "Your gran really misses you." Just act as if nothing was unusual at all. She didn't want to embarrass the boy.

Rubberbones didn't seem surprised to see her. "Er, hello, Miss Em. Not doin' too well, really. Nobody wants to see me bounce."

"Gosh. You'd think anyone would. Can I throw this brick at you?"

"I'd be glad if you did."

Emmaline picked up a half brick and flung it at Rubberbones. It hit his chest and bounced onto the floor. He didn't seem to be hurt, but it wasn't a very hard toss either. She tried again, with a stronger throw, and the result was the same.

"It's not very impressive, Rab. I mean, I'm glad it doesn't hurt, but, well, what's the point?"

"You're right, Miss Em." The boy was quite miserable. "The Gypsies don't want me to hurt meself. I tried jumping out of a tree for sixpence, but they just stopped me and gave the man his money back."

"You know," said Emmaline, "I'd be very happy for you to jump out of the tree in our garden anytime you want. Or off the roof. And we'd pay you by the day. Or the tree, if you prefer!"

"You'd take me back, then?" gasped Rab. Emmaline thought he seemed relieved.

"Why, of course! Why ever would you think we wouldn't?" Emmaline was puzzled.

"'Cos I smashed up the flyer, Miss Em. 'Cos it were yours and it were fantastic and I broke it, and I knew all about the football match and I lied to you!"

"*You* smashed up the flying machine?" Emmaline didn't understand.

"Aye. It were so beautiful, an' flew so true, an' it were

your pride and joy. I could tell. But I smashed it up. I don't exactly remember what 'appened. I landed, it seemed fine, and then suddenly I bumped me 'ead a little bit. And then I saw the machine all destroyed. I knew you'd be heartbroke, so I run off."

"My goodness, Robert Burns!" exclaimed Emmaline. "You flew straight and true. You landed perfectly. You didn't smash the machine up at all."

"Then how — who — ?" Rubberbones was wide-eyed and stammering.

"That was your football friends. The ball hit you on the head. They rushed over and trampled the flyer with you inside. It wasn't your fault at all."

The boy beamed. Emmaline grinned back at him.

"Come on, Rab. Let's go and say good-bye to the Gypsies."

Rubberbones followed Emmaline toward the cart. Lal Singh was entertaining a handful of Romany children, playing a strange eastern melody on a tin flute. Stranger still, a worm was swaying upward out of a tin can at his feet.

"Not so fast, youngling!" called out the Gypsy chief. "You can't leave yet!"

Behind them, the muscular *barossan* stood with his arms folded.

CHAPTER 7

Grubby Hands and Prophecies

The chief smiled at Emmaline and Rubberbones. "You cannot go before you have your fortunes foretold!"

So the two would-be aeronauts followed the old man into a tent where a sign announced that "MADAME ZAZA TELLS THY *FORTUNE*. MARRIAGE! INHERITANCE! THE LAWS OF FATE REVEALED!"

The inside of the tent was swathed in veils of purple cloth. Madame ZaZa was hunched over a crystal ball. She and the table were draped in swirling lengths of sequinned fabric.

"Mornin', Sid!" croaked the old woman.

"Give these two a reading, Norah. On the 'ouse. Nice kids. Want a cuppa tea?" asked the chief. He put on a pair of fluffy bedroom slippers and reading glasses.

"Smashing. And a bacon sandwich, if there's one going!" called out the Romany Seeress of the Vienna Woods (as was declared on the side of her wagon). "And a bit o' chocolate cake."

Emmaline thought this discussion lacked something in the way of mystical Eastern flavor. Still, how often did you get your future foretold by a real Gypsy?

Emmaline thought they must be genuine. Fakers would not call each other "Sid" and "Norah" when outsiders were present. They wouldn't ask for tea and bacon sandwiches and chocolate cake.

Rab and Emmaline sat down. Sid brought in a plate of chocolate cake for them all to share. The fortune-teller wolfed down a sandwich.

"Let's 'ave a look at yer 'ands, then!" commanded Madame ZaZa, still chewing. The youngsters did as they were told. Emmaline's hands were considerably cleaner than Rab's.

"Lifeline's quite strong, dearie," the fortune-teller announced as she held Emmaline's right hand up for inspection. "I don't know as you'll live to be much more than ninety, but you'll certainly live long enough to be a ruddy nuisance to yer grandchildren!" Madame ZaZa cackled.

"You're a very bright girl," she went on. "You march to the beat of your own horn, right enough. Folks think you're a bit odd, do they? Probably right, I suppose, but 'oo cares? You 'ave a great future, if you stay true to yourself. But there are many obstacles in your way."

"Obstacles, Madame ZaZa?" asked Emmaline.

"Yes, stumblin' blocks. Some are people trying to stop you doin' what you 'ave to do. Some are fizzical things like rain and forests and stuff like that. And some of them are inside you. Those are the most difficult ones, really."

"You mean, the ones inside me are the hardest to overcome?"

"Well, yeah, of course. Them and the monsters. And the men wiv masks."

"What!" Emmaline was alarmed. "You see those in my future?"

"No, 'course not, dearie. Just 'avin' a laugh," chuckled Madame ZaZa. "I'm just sayin' that some things are harder to overcome than others. Didn't mean to frighten you, my duck." She smiled, showing gold, white and black teeth.

Emmaline let out her breath as she took back her shaking hand. The old Gypsy woman took Rubberbones by his grimy front paw.

"Good Lord!" exclaimed Madame ZaZa. "You've got

the longest, strongest lifeline I've ever seen. You could wrestle bears and come out 'ealthier for having the exercise. You could be run over by a train and hardly even notice. You'll live to be a thousand!"

"Really?" Rubberbones's jaw dropped.

"Well, p'raps not a thousand. But a good long life in amazin' fit fashion. You'll probably fall off a cliff when you're hunting for gulls' eggs on your hundred-and-fifteenth birthday."

Rubberbones made a mental note to spend all his birthdays after a hundred and fourteen quietly indoors. He was a very literal sort of boy.

The Gypsy was tracing the mucky creases of Rab's palm. "Wait a minute. 'Ang on 'ere. Let's see that again. A very unusual boy, yes. You have a special talent. Somethin' very strange, in fact. No, that makes no sense —"

"What makes no sense?" asked Emmaline.

"The reading makes no sense," replied Madame ZaZa. "This lad is what we call a natural or an 'instinctive.' Someone 'oo can easily do something wot most people can't. You get violinists and artists as 'ave what most of us think of as amazin' powers, but come just as easy as blinking to themselves. This lad's got the same thing — except that his skill isn't possible at all. It says that he can fly."

Rubberbones looked at her blankly. Emmaline wasn't certain what the old woman meant. Could he just . . . fly?

Madame ZaZa waved at the lad. "Go ahead, son. Jump in the air and flap your wings."

So, being an easygoing and obliging sort of boy, he did. Nothing happened. Well, he jumped in the air and flapped his arms. He just looked silly.

Rubberbones did not fly. He tried jumping and flapping with greater effort and energy. Still nothing.

The Gypsy woman seemed mystified. She looked at one youngster, then the other. She gasped and seized both Emmaline and Rubberbones by the hands, pulling them together. She inspected both right palms. A long line crossed from one hand to the other.

"Goodness! You, my lad, can fly — but only with your aid, my girl. You can create something that travels through air — but you cannot do it without this little fellow. Your *destinies are linked* in this matter. Your *fates are interwoven* for this purpose."

The fortune-teller had the Gypsy Seeress voice on, all of a sudden. There was grandeur in her manner. She seemed to tap into the ancient wisdom of her wandering people as she intoned her prophecy. All the mystery of Romany lore hung heavily in the atmosphere.

"Now, would you like a bit o' this excellent chocolate cake?" asked Madame ZaZa, as she dabbed bacon grease off her jingling bracelet.

But Emmaline thought she could see fear in the old woman's eyes.

CHAPTER 8

The Strictest School in the World

Emmaline and Rubberbones were eager to rebuild the flyer as soon as they returned home. But by then it was time for Emmaline to leave for her new school. It was, in fact, her only school; Emmaline had always been taught by a governess and private tutors. This school didn't sound promising from the letter she'd received. Still, as Aunt Lucy said, it might turn out well enough.

Although she hadn't seemed convinced herself, even as she said it.

Rubberbones said it would be "a lark, what wi' all them other lasses. Yer'll 'ave a right laff."

Emmaline's experience with "other lasses" had not involved anything she could call a right laugh. Or any kind of laugh. The daughters of her parents' friends in India were prim, proper and snooty to a high degree.

The school was fifty miles from Lower Owlthwaite, and the sensible thing would have been to drive the dog cart to the railway station at Groansby, take a train, change at Leeds, take another train to a local station, then a cab up to the school. That would be the sensible thing to do.

They decided to take the dogcart all the way. A dog cart is not really intended for that. First of all, they aren't pulled by dogs at all. They are for dogs to ride in, hunting dogs on their way to venues for, well, chasing smaller animals. (Aunt

Lucy didn't hold with that sort of thing, of course.) The cart was tall, with a seat facing forward and a lower one behind it facing backward over what amounted to a kennel. It was pulled by an elderly horse called Ernest. All in all, the dogcart was a jolly, quite exciting way of getting about the villages nearby. It was a terribly uncomfortable way of taking a girl, her aunt, a small boy and a dignified Indian butler, plus a trunk of clothes, for a two-day trip to the coast.

Aunt Lucy forgot this until after they'd got down the long hill out of Lower Owlthwaite. She gave Ernest a nettle-and-greenfly sandwich and patted his nose. "There will be a bag of carrots at the end of this, my boy."

Ernest did not seem to think it was worth the effort. He spat out the sandwich and trod on it.

Rubberbones knew it, too, and though he weighed less than Emmaline's loaded trunk, he decided that his extra weight was unfair to Ernest.

"Good-bye, Miss Em. I'll see you at the Christmas 'olidays. We'll go flying again then. Landing in t'snow must be grand!" He ran off up the hill. Emmaline waved sadly; he turned and waved back.

"Good-bye, Rab!" she called out, knowing he couldn't hear.

The towers loomed out of the mist like some medieval stronghold. There were two of them, and they could be seen at a great distance, before the squat bulk of the walls came into view. The massive building was fearsome. It was menacing. It was

ST. GRIMELDA'S SCHOOL FOR YOUNG LADIES, EST. 1552

The brass plaque shone amid the huge gray stones and heavy, studded door.

Emmaline studied the rocky vastness of the school. There was no ivy to mellow the sheer grayness of the walls. At the

top of each great tower there was a battlement, where archers left over from the Middle Ages could shoot at anyone coming up the long driveway, say, in a dogcart.

Nothing moved. No one could be seen.

Lal Singh banged on a cast-iron knocker the size of a dustbin lid.

A grating slid open, at about the height of Lal Singh's stomach. Beady eyes in a pale, pinched face looked out. "You'd be the new girl, then?"

It was obvious that the tall, bearded Indian man was not the new girl, but everyone knew what the gatekeeper meant. He emerged from a small doorway cut into the massive gates, brandishing a huge bunch of keys as if they were a badge of his importance. He was a quarter of an inch taller than Aunt Lucy, making him almost five feet in height. He was beaky, bald and much taken with his own complaints. That was obvious.

As he pottered and dithered about with the keys, a sharp voice rang out from behind. "Pinchbeak, do stop pottering

and dithering about. Bring the new gel along to me, then get her things while I escort her to see Mrs. Wackett."

A very tall, severe-looking woman met them at the gates. She appeared to have washed her face with a scouring pad every morning. "My name is Miss Scantcommon. You can call me Matron. Your, ah, guardian can come along, too. Your servant can help Mr. Pinchbeak with your things. We shall report to the headmistress."

Emmaline offered her hand in politeness. The woman ignored it, turning crisply on her heel and striding away.

Emmaline was shocked. The woman had called Lal Singh a servant! And she expected Aunt Lucy to run along behind like a puppy. Emmaline fumed. Yet all she could do was follow Miss Scantcommon across the cobbled yard.

The study was large. The polished oak desk was large. The woman behind it was larger still. She looked like a mountain that had been stuffed into a tweed suit and sensible shoes. Her hair was dark, her eyes were black, her spectacles were balanced at the end of her nose. She smiled at Emmaline. She had the kind of smile you'd expect from a crocodile.

There were two hard, narrow-backed chairs in front of the desk, contrasting with the overstuffed cushioned chair that the vast and sinister figure behind it occupied.

"Miss Cayley. I am Mrs. Wackett, and this is my school. Please sit down."

Aunt Lucy sat down, or rather climbed up, for the chair was designed for a much taller and thinner person. Emmaline sat as well.

Mrs. Wackett went straight to the point. "I have a letter from your mother. A rather mealy-mouthed woman. What she says, if I understand her silly waffling, is that you've never had any proper schooling or discipline, you associate with unsuitable people and you need to be taken in hand.

You have strange, unhealthy interests quite unsuited to a gel of your station in life. You know nothing of proper manners for a lady, despite what your mother claims are her own best efforts. I take it that's about the size of it?"

Emmaline gulped. What an incredibly rude woman!

Mrs. Wackett's eyes moved toward Aunt Lucy, in the way a giant lizard might notice an insect. "You'd be the *aunt*, then? Mrs. Cayley indicates that you are hardly the ideal influence on her daughter. Nevertheless, since both parents are in India, it seems wise to have at least some sort of relative available in case of death, debilitating injury, fatal illness, that sort of thing."

Aunt Lucy said nothing. This was because she had learned to gulp silently.

Mrs. Wackett continued. "We at St. Grimelda's pride ourselves in being firm. Very firm. The school was founded as a convent for difficult young nuns with large fortunes. That was a very long time ago, of course, and we no longer use the rack or the iron maiden as part of ordinary school discipline. Not necessary. In the time of Henry the Eighth, the convent became a girls' school; the king wanted to knock the place down, but he was . . . persuaded otherwise. He died, and his son gave us a charter. We have been here a long time. And we are honored to be considered the strictest school for girls in the world. There's a place in Germany that claims to be as strict, but I know for certain they have to use all kinds of restraining devices and medieval punishments — stocks, pillories, that sort of thing. We don't need to do that here! Everyone knows that they must follow the rules, and we have no difficulty whatsoever keeping everyone in line."

Mrs. Wackett went over a list of rules. It seemed that everything that was not forbidden was compulsory. Hats had to be worn at certain times and places, but at other times wearing a hat would be punishable. Likewise, running was against the rules in hallways but obligatory on the playing field. A bewildering list of things that *should not*, *must not*, and *must at all times* went by in a flurry of Mrs. Wackett's crisp pronouncements.

There were two final instructions.

"Your parents would prefer that you remain at the school during holidays. I think you'll find our Christmas celebrations quite sober and respectable."

Emmaline gawped.

"Finally, you will be allowed to write to your aunt, of course, although we do monitor what the girls pass along in their letters — avoids a lot of foolishness. However, we don't encourage visits; they upset those girls who have nobody to come and see them."

Aunt Lucy was close to tears. Emmaline felt numb all

over. The woman whom they called Matron came and took Emmaline by the arm.

"I'll show you the dormitory now."

Mrs. Wackett smiled tightly. "You may say good-bye to your aunt, if you aren't too long about it."

Aunt Lucy tried to put on a brave face. "It can't be that bad, Em, dear. Your mother wouldn't have chosen a horrid place for your education."

Emmaline frowned at the thought. Her mother wouldn't, would she?

"Write and let us know how you settle in, dear."

Aunt Lucy hugged her niece around the waist. Emmaline, a head taller, patted her aunt's shoulders and tried not to cry.

Miss Scantcommon led Emmaline through severe corridors and dark foyers, up frowning staircases and down forbidding hallways to the dormitory. Beds, made up with joyless efficiency, were lined up along the whitewashed walls. At the end of the room were a table and hard-looking benches, all splinters and discomfort. A group of girls were gathered, poring over books or scribbling away on paper.

"Gels, this is Emmaline Cayley. Emmaline, this is the Upper Middle."

The Upper Middle (whatever that meant) consisted of a number of girls about Emmaline's age, clad in the severe clothes that St. Grimelda's demanded.

"I'll leave you gels to let Emmaline know . . . what she needs to know."

"What I'm in for, is what she means," thought Emmaline as Matron's heels clipped sharply down the hallway.

The Upper Middle introduced themselves. At least, some of them did. A girl with blond curls spoke for those who didn't have anything to say. Her name was Amelia, which she pronounced carefully, as if it would break if not treated delicately.

Petunia and Petronella were fair-haired twins almost as impressed with themselves as with Amelia. Emmaline knew right away they were Amelia's chorus, expected to agree with her and laugh at her jokes.

Gwendolyn sat close to Amelia and gave the firm impression that she was some sort of bodyguard. She frowned fiercely.

Margaret was crying softly.

Jane was crying loudly.

Anna was stonily silent.

Hannah smiled encouragingly. "Hello, Emmaline," she said.

Princess Purnah had dark eyes and wild hair. Whether she was really a princess was not clear, as she sat in silence. Amelia claimed that the girl's father was "The Grand Poohbah of Humpty-Dumpty." The twins smirked as if this were very funny indeed. Princess Purnah said nothing, but Emmaline could have sworn she glimpsed a flicker of anger cross her face. Amelia continued, "She's been here three years and doesn't speak a word of the language. You'd think she'd have picked it up. She must be unusually stupid, even for a foreigner."

Mary-Alice giggled at Amelia's remark. She had been giggling throughout. Emmaline thought she might be hysterical, as if she were trying so hard to appear cheerful that it had turned her a bit mad.

Emmaline hated Amelia right away. She clenched her teeth to avoid saying so.

"You'll get used to the school," Amelia continued. "Everyone does, in her own way." She waved airily at her classmates. Emmaline wondered if crying or giggling madly were their own ways of getting used to St. Grimelda's.

"This is the class, except for Bernadette. She's being punished, and we don't discuss that," Amelia said. "Mrs. Wackett is ghastly, of course, but you can work your way around her. Sucking up can help, if you are good at it. She loves to be horridly strict and frighten people — so it helps if she thinks you are frightened. Look at this lot here." She gestured at the other girls. "Most of them really *are* terrified. If you see someone doing anything she shouldn't, report her immediately. It'll get her in trouble, of course, but it will put you in well with the Wackett."

She looked at Emmaline with cold blue eyes. "So, if I see you up to anything, I shall turn you in. If you catch me breaking the rules, you can turn me in, as you wish. But of course you won't."

Emmaline wondered what *that* meant. That she'd never catch Amelia going against the many, many rules of St. Grimelda's? Or that she'd never have the nerve to turn her in?

Amelia smirked. The twins smirked. The big, plain girl known as Gwendolyn cracked her knuckles loudly. Amelia went on. "Punishments here are ... different. They make you clean out the birds."

That didn't sound too horrible, thought Emmaline. But with this remark even stonily silent Anna began to blubber. Margaret fainted, knocking over her chair.

CHAPTER 9

A Dickensian Sort of Chapter

Over the next few days Emmaline found out more about her new school.

The classes were given odd names. The youngest girls were known as the "Shells." Then came the "Removes." Emmaline was in the "Upper Middle." There was no "Lower Middle." Rumor had it they'd been eaten by rats. There were fourth and fifth forms above them. Each class (or "form") had ten or twelve girls, who shared a dorm like the one she slept in. The beds were hard and narrow with an exact distance of two feet, nine inches, between them.

Most schools that Emmaline knew about had "houses," where older girls mixed with younger ones and helped them along. To show leadership toward the newer pupils. To have healthy competition in team sports. At St. Grimelda's there weren't any houses. There was no emphasis on working together. Perhaps that was why the girls didn't help one another or have any sense of being part of a team.

There were lots of things that Emmaline found out day by day. The baths were cold. Arctic cold. Shivering-walrus cold. Matron called it "character building" when she refused Emmaline an extra towel; the towels were the size of hand-kerchiefs, with a surface like sandpaper.

There were smells so ancient — like medieval toilets,

milk left in the sun and mice that had died in the cellar — that no disinfectant could defeat them. Scrubbing made no difference. The girls had to sweep, dust, polish and mop every morning before lessons began. There were staff for cooking and laundry duties, old and bad-tempered women from the surrounding villages. The cook was terrible; her food was even worse than Aunt Lucy's. Emmaline knew that if Aunt Lucy gave you slug salad, it was fresh and properly washed. She had no idea what the gray, chewy stuff was that Cook served in pies and stew. And she knew that boiled potatoes were supposed to be softer than pebbles.

Emmaline had always liked to read novels and to compare the stories with her own life. St. Grimelda's made her think of the novels of Charles Dickens, with their slum conditions, mean relations, dashed hopes and general aspects of brutal misery (and miserable brutality). But they were cheery tales compared with daily life at St. Grimelda's.

The girls themselves were beastly to one another. Since almost nothing enjoyable was allowed, girls tried to hide small things, like sweets and trinkets. Every piece of this "contraband" — as if it were smuggler's cargo — would be seized by older girls.

Emmaline heard a fourth-form girl boasting to a friend: "I took this ribbon off some nasty little Remove. She'd hidden it in her pocket, but I saw it and twisted her arm 'til she gave over —"

The following day she overheard the same girl complaining to the same friend in the hallway. "Some ghastly bully in the fifth form pinched my ribbon, the shrew. She twisted my arm like a fiend until I was forced to let her have it —"

Amelia and her friend Gwendolyn — "the bodyguard" as Hannah referred to her — were especially good at the business of bullying, confiscating and general beastliness.

Nobody ever took anything from Amelia. Her sharp tongue and Gwendolyn's cracking knuckles saw to that. On the second day, Emmaline saw Amelia force Anna to hand over a piece of cake. It wasn't that she wanted the cake. Amelia didn't eat it. She just wanted to display her power.

Strangely, although the girls spent a lot of effort being horrible to one another, they were extremely — in fact, weirdly — obedient to the teachers, especially Mrs. Wackett and Matron. Teachers simply reminded girls of "the consequences of misbehavior," and the girls shuddered, turned pale and jumped to attention. Or fainted.

The girl known as Bernadette had finally returned from her punishment. Nobody would talk about what she'd done to be punished, or what that punishment had been. Bernadette herself seemed unlikely to say. She was a pale girl whose hair appeared to have turned the color of dirty chalk. This was odd for a fourteen-year-old girl. She sat eerily silent or talked to herself about butterflies. Emmaline did not see this as being a good sign for Bernadette.

Education was one thing. Imprisonment was another. Emmaline had to find a way out of St. Grimelda's. She had a flying machine to invent, and this, surely, was no place to do that.

———

Dearest Mama,

Emmaline thought this was a silly way of addressing her mother, but Mrs. Cayley was that sort of person. Frilly. Roses and bows and eau de cologne. Emmaline sometimes felt bad that she had no time for the things her mother thought were important. Mrs. Cayley wanted her daughter to learn ladylike things; obvi-ously, Emmaline's mother had no idea what a harsh place St. Grimelda's actually was. So Emmaline decided to tell her.

I have been here at St. Grimelda's for a week now, and I must tell you that it is the most frightful institution you can imagine. It is like a prison for girls. The headmistress is a dragon! The staff are like guards! The food is hideous! The other girls are terrified out of their wits! There are bullies, who work out their frustrations on the younger and smaller girls —

Hannah was looking over her shoulder. "You know the Wicked Wackett will never let you send that letter, don't you? They read all correspondence before it goes out."

Of course, Hannah was right. There was no chance a letter telling the truth about St. Grimelda's was going to pass the censorship of her captors.

So Emmaline wrote another letter. She took out all the bad stuff, which left almost nothing in it at all. It was a general greeting to her mother to indicate that she was alive and remembered how to write a letter. It seemed rather pointless. She wrote another one, with at least a sense of real affection, to Aunt Lucy. It said nothing about the school, but it was a letter home. She finished it:

And give my very best to Lal Singh and Rab.

"Home," Emmaline thought to herself. The strange old house on the hill felt like home.

Rubberbones found that he could not go back to the world he had known just a short time ago. He still lived with his gran, and still did odd jobs for whoever needed them. Miss Aunt Lucy kept sending for him to do little things, and he was happy to go. But he found that he was never happy to be there, even if she paid him far too much to run errands and dig turnips, because he missed Miss Em. Miss Aunt

Lucy also missed Miss Em. A lot. That was clear. She moped about and rearranged her jars of jellied snails along the top of the piano. Even Lal Singh seemed less jaunty than before. His mustache drooped at the ends.

Rubberbones also missed flying. It was a world that had opened up to him suddenly, and then — with Emmaline's departure — disappeared.

He could never fly again. Or could he?

Two weeks after Emmaline left for St. Grimelda's, Rubberbones brought the remains of the flyer out from the old stable. He spread the mangled pieces on the ground. Some of the bits were good, mostly the small brass and iron fittings. The cloth was ripped only in a few places, though the tears were long and nasty. It was the wooden struts and supports that had been destroyed.

But wood was easy to come by. And the same tools and pots of glue they had used before were still there.

Even after he racked his brain, Rab couldn't remember how it all fitted together.

That was when Lal Singh came in with Emmaline's book. And the saws, drills, glue and other tools in a big box marked "Flying Machine."

"You'll be wanting some tea and a piece of my fish, treacle and onion cake while we are working," said Aunt Lucy, bringing in a tray with three cups and plates.

———

Emmaline found Latin boring but frightening, an unusual combination caused by Miss Venividivici's frequent rapping of a ruler across the knuckles of any girl she noticed talking, or shuffling, or not knowing her irregular verbs. This was especially disturbing to Emmaline as she had known no Latin verbs at all when she arrived at St. Grimelda's. Emmaline had never really bothered learning anything that

didn't interest her before now. However, her keen mind and fear of pain helped her learn thirty-seven irregular verbs inside a week.

In Miss Sumfiddle's mathematics class, in Miss Chalkfruit's sketching group and on the games court with Miss Sharpelbow, Emmaline had one thing on her mind. (Well, actually, two if you count "avoiding potential crippling injury," for the games were rough.)

Escape.

"How can I get a secret letter out of here?" she asked Hannah one night after a bruising day of games and Latin verbs.

Hannah thought for a while. "Girls have tried to bribe the cook and the laundrywoman. Those two'll turn you in right away. They're as frightened of Wackett as we are. Girls who go home for the holidays are searched for contraband; only those girls who are convinced that they should keep their mouths shut are allowed to go. They won't help at all. So, I don't know. I've never heard of anyone managing it."

Emmaline thought of the ways people in stories passed messages.

Notes in bottles, thrown into the sea.

Pieces of paper slipped inside library books.

Friendly tramps bribed with pieces of bacon.

Carrier pigeons.

"Aha!" said Emmaline. "What about carrier pigeons? I could get —"

"The birds would get them," said Hannah.

The birds?

The bell rang for lights-out.

The reconstructed flyer didn't look much different from the model that had soared from the church tower. There were new sections of fabric — a calico tablecloth in this case, which added "a lovely dash of color" in the opinion of Aunt Lucy — and woodwork that was freshly cut and glued in place. They had followed the plans carefully. It had taken four days of steady effort. Rubberbones thought it looked like the old flyer. He was pretty sure it was the same. Lal Singh worked silently, but Rab could see that the spark was missing from his efforts.

"To the church, do you think?" asked Aunt Lucy.

Lal Singh said nothing.

"Quite right. Don't want to be seen by the public yet. The roof, then."

"Champion!" said Rubberbones with a chipper note to his voice that he didn't quite feel. Aunt Lucy looked at him, and he thought there was a worried edge to her smile.

St. Grimelda's didn't welcome visitors, but there was one exception. Every Wednesday morning a delivery wagon came in from the nearby village, Fishwick, with sacks of flour, tubs of butter and so forth. The grocer and his boy always left the van — a four-wheeled cart with "Thos. Appleburr, Groceries and Provisions, Established 1867" stenciled on the side — while they unloaded the cargo. The carthorse was old and unlikely to go anywhere, except home when he was told to. He usually snorted in an elderly, complaining way and thought about carrots.

This Wednesday morning, Emmaline was awaiting her chance. The bell between classes signaled her to report to Miss Screechleigh's choral hour. Instead, she hid in one of St. Grimelda's gloomy alcoves waiting for the courtyard to empty. Then she slipped swiftly and silently under the wagon. Emmaline heard the grocer and his lad climbing up onto the seats. Matron was talking; Emmaline could make out the words "Good money for bad flour" and the grocer muttering in reply. She gripped the front axle with her hands, pushing her feet tightly against the rear axle. Three weeks of gymnastic humiliation from Miss Sharpelbow had given her some strength in the arms and shoulders. She could hold on. She had to hold on if she were ever to escape.

She fell off. The horse had only moved a few feet. The van had twisted and jolted amazingly for something that was going slower than a wheelbarrow.

She lay in the courtyard, in a puddle. The only puddle.

Miss Scantcommon stood overhead, glowering at her.

The grocer's boy laughed, until the grocer clipped his ear.

Amelia and her friends looked down from their classroom window, pointing and giggling at Emmaline.

Rubberbones and Lal Singh carried the flying machine up to the roof, as before. And Rab flew it straight into the tree, as before. Aunt Lucy sighed.

Something was missing. "It's not right!" said Rab, from twenty feet above the ground, with twigs in his hair.

As Rubberbones slipped out from the belt that was holding him upside down, he said what they all knew: "We need Miss Em. It don't work wi'out her."

Then he let go, falling in a heap and bouncing right up again as he always did.

If they needed Miss Em, Miss Em felt that she needed them. She wasn't doing very well on her own.

Her brilliant escape plan had been attempted before, actually about once a month since the school was founded. There were rules to the escape game. It was understood that nobody was to peer underneath and say, "You're caught, my gel," or anything of that sort until the wagon started moving and the girl fell off. That was all part of the fun.

The girl almost always fell off within a few feet of starting. Once a girl had made it through the gates and got halfway to the village. That was in 1644.

"Lots of girls are killed when the wagon runs over them," said Hannah afterwards. "Old Pinchbeak buries them in a pit out on the moor. It's those who survive that I feel sorry for."

Emmaline was almost certain that her friend was talking nonsense. But she did worry about what the punishment would be. When Pinchbeak appeared, a shudder of fear ran through her.

The porter led Emmaline to a bare chamber. A tiny window looked out onto the kitchen wastebins. A pen and a scroll of blank paper lay on a spindly old desk that had had initials carved onto it by generations of children. She could make out the markings "AAAGH 1765." After an hour, Miss Scantcommon came in, all strictness and starched collar.

"Emmaline Susan Jane Cayley. You will write out the phrase 'Should I ever again attempt to leave St. Grimelda's without proper permission, I will clean out the birds.' Do it one hundred times in your best copperplate handwriting." Miss Scantcommon scowled at her, then marched out of the room, locking the door behind her.

Emmaline wrote the words out as she had been told. It wasn't a terrible punishment. It just made no sense.

CHAPTER 10

The Ball Game

Rubberbones was adding a variety of strange and unlikely plant life to Aunt Lucy's stew pot when the letter from St. Grimelda's arrived. So he was able to watch when Aunt Lucy tore it open and read the brief page from Emmaline. Aunt Lucy's face was grim.

"Something is wrong with Emmaline. This school — well, there is clearly something terribly amiss."

Rubberbones didn't say things like "terribly amiss," but he understood that something was wrong.

"What's it say, Miss Aunt Lucy?" he asked.

"It's what it doesn't say, I think. It is polite. Emmaline hopes I am well. She is well. She is in something called an Upper Middle. There are other girls there. She has classes, apparently taught by teachers. It all reads like a letter written by somebody who is being watched over her shoulder, if you get my meaning. No, something isn't right."

Lal Singh appeared. Aunt Lucy turned to him.

"We are going to that school to see exactly what's going on. The staff won't be happy to see us. I expect they'll give us some kind of fobbing-off. That headmistress is an ogre. So bring a few extra bits and bobs as may come in useful."

Then she turned to Rubberbones.

"Robert. Do you know that kite you used to float up around the chimneys with? Please fetch it, with as long a piece of rope as you can manage."

The sports ground was not a green field as it was in most schools. Instead, it was a small courtyard off the main quad, surrounded by walls the height of a tall man or a very tall schoolgirl. The only sport played was the Ball Game, which had been part of St. Grimelda's history since before anyone could remember. Like the usual girls' game of field hockey it involved sticks and a ball, but everything else about it was different. The goals were alcoves carved into the center of the walls on all four sides. This was because the game was played with four teams of four girls and three balls in play at once. The object was to score as many goals (or "buckets") as you could in any of the other teams' alcoves (or "caves"). You had to protect against buckets in your own cave. You could use the stick to knock the ball along or to trip other players. You could hit other players across the shins or knees. You could bounce the ball off the walls as often as you liked. You weren't allowed to carry the ball by hand or hide it inside your uniform. No punching or biting was allowed. Not much, anyway. Some hair pulling was permitted. If Miss Sharpelbow decided you'd broken one of the very few rules, you'd be told to climb up and sit on top of the wall for a count of 100.

The Ball Game reminded Emmaline of the strangely medieval football match between the Owlthwaite villages. Except that at St. Grimelda's there was more squealing and hair pulling, less grunting and shoving. And the girls were more savage.

Emmaline hated it immediately.

Yet she still had to play. It was compulsory. "Builds character!" bellowed Miss Sharpelbow.

Teams were picked in the traditional way. The games mistress chose her favorites — muscular girls of seemingly low intelligence and ferocious attitude — to be team captains. They chose their friends. Then they selected girls who weren't their friends but who looked large or athletic or bad-tempered, or all three. Then they chose everyone else, down to the extremely shortsighted, overweight or otherwise physically underequipped.

Emmaline hated the choosing even more than the game itself. She hated it when some already selected loud-mouthed girls talked about a particularly short, round girl from the Removes as a "dwarf" and a "midget." And she hated herself for hoping she would at least get picked before that tiny, chubby, now-crying child.

Miss Sharpelbow, however, loved the Ball Game very much, and it was a great disappointment to her that no other schools played it. This might be because of the appalling level of violent injury that the game involved. (Most parents do not send their gently nurtured daughters to an expensive school to have their arms bitten; after all, younger brothers and sisters will do that at home for nothing.)

This morning, Emmaline belonged to a team led by a hulking young lady with a broken nose and legs like tree trunks who actually seemed to like playing the Ball Game. Her name was Josie Pinner. She reminded Emmaline of Frankenstein's monster — except a bit fiercer.

The game started. Josie led from the front, shoving opponents out of the way. Emmaline moved along behind her. Miss Sharpelbow believed that the best way of refereeing a game was to let the girls do whatever they wanted, blowing her whistle only when the pile of bodies got unusually high. Josie scored lots of buckets, and her bruising presence kept most other players from getting close to her own cave. Some girls would try to hit the ball from a long distance, but nobody would come near. Even the strongest, toughest girls avoided close contact with Josie.

Emmaline had no idea of the score. That wasn't on her mind at all. She just wanted to get through the class without being maimed.

So, quite why she did it, Emmaline couldn't explain.

What happened was this. Josie was charging toward the cave directly in front of her. Girls scattered. A small, blond girl named Charlotte from the Removes, twelve years old but looking nine, did not scatter. She was rooted to the spot. Fear was in her eyes. Death — or at least considerable damage — was in her immediate future. Josie did not stop. Josie quite probably did not even see her.

Knuckle-cracking Gwendolyn stepped in front of her tiny teammate, stick gripped tight.

Charlotte, finding the most unhelpful thing to do, clutched the larger girl from behind. They both overbalanced.

All the other girls held their breath. Miss Sharpelbow blew her whistle. But the pea inside it had jammed. A single pathetic peep, heard by no one, came out. Josie's eyes were on the ball, bouncing a step ahead of her. Two steps ahead, Gwendolyn and Charlotte were tangled in a heap of arms and legs.

So Emmaline did what anyone would do. Anyone who didn't want to live to see another school dinner. She lunged forward and hooked her stick under Josie's ankle.

There was a humongous crash, like a great oak falling in a forest. Emmaline leaped out of the way. Gwendolyn and Charlotte untangled and rolled aside.

Miss Sharpelbow's whistle suddenly came unstopped and blasted shrilly. The gym teacher hadn't expected this, but a whistle always signaled a foul. She immediately ruled against Emmaline for "unsporting conduct," and made her climb up on the wall for a count of five hundred. Josie got up, rubbed her ankle, snarled a bit and carried on with her usual fierce determination.

Amelia had a few words after the game. She might have been happy that Emmaline had saved her friend Gwendolyn from injury, but that wasn't what she had to say.

"Emmaline, you've made an enemy in Josie. Rough girl. Common. I'd watch out if I were you. But, fortunately, I'm not you."

It was late in the day when Rubberbones, atop the dogcart, first spotted the towers of St. Grimelda's. Along the way, Aunt Lucy and Lal Singh had concocted a plan.

A plan that would work best at night.

They didn't go up to the gates to argue with the grumpy caretaker. Instead, they took the curving track downhill toward Fishwick, the village that sat below the cliffs and looked out onto the North Sea.

Aunt Lucy picked a hotel — "Sunshine View" — and arranged rooms for herself, Lal Singh and Rab. While Lal Singh attended to Ernest, the horse, Aunt Lucy chatted with the landlord. Rubberbones sat quietly, nursing a glass of lemonade, and watched as Aunt Lucy peppered him with questions.

"Interesting village, Fishwick," said Aunt Lucy. "I hear there's a famous girls' school here."

"Aye. Strange place. My sister knows the woman who works in the kitchen there, an' she says it's full of secrets. My brother-in-law used to deliver meat to the school, years ago, and he said there were 'things up there that'd curl yer beard.'"

"Secrets, landlord?" asked Aunt Lucy. She had ordered a

glass of sherry and told him to have a drink for himself. Rubberbones listened, trying to look like a servant boy (easy enough) and not a bold aeronaut with a kite of his own.

"Aye, madam. Many secrets. It's an old building, with a cliff on one side and those towers as looms up out of the fog. Not a happy place. They say that there are strange noises over the moors at night. Nobody goes in or out for days at a time, 'cept for deliveries and village women as works up there."

"So there are women who go up there daily?"

"Not very willingly, I'd tell ye, missus. Them as works there is them as can't get a situation in the village. There's a cook and a couple of laundry maids. Nobody wants to work there if they 'ave a choice in t'matter. They go up first thing, come back afore it gets dark. Won't be out on the moors after nightfall." The landlord was enjoying his story.

"Goodness! Why not? The fog? Losing their way home?" asked Aunt Lucy. She made her eyes as big as saucers.

"Aye, that, no doubt. But there's always been talk of some odd creatures out at night; I heard some tales from my grandfather, an' he from his. Folks say there's deviltry

about," said the landlord with relish.

"No! What? Wolves? Bears? Ghostly hounds?" Miss Aunt Lucy was leading him on. She was clever, she was, said Rab to himself. "Werewolves, vampires, that sort of thing?"

Rubberbones's eyes grew large themselves as he considered the prospect of meeting vampires.

The landlord shook his head and leaned forward. "Birds," he whispered. "They say there's birds as is kept in one o' them school towers. Always has been, ever since anyone remembers."

"Strange, frightening birds?" thought Rubberbones. "What could they be? Owls? Eagles? There aren't any eagles round these parts, are there? And, anyway, eagles aren't a threat to folk. Naw, this must be one of them old country tales that mothers frighten their young 'uns with.

"Surely?"

Lal Singh and Rubberbones crept out of the hotel carrying a very large, flat parcel in the middle of the night. (It was actually only about eight o'clock. Fishwick was a quiet village, and the local people had been in bed for hours.) They went on foot across the moor by moonlight. There was enough wind to keep the fog away, and to fly a kite. Most people don't happen to be carrying a kite on dark moorlands fifty miles from home, of course. But Rubberbones was. He had brought his original brown-paper-and-strapping-tape kite with some extra bits of shaped wood and fabric salvaged from the last flying machine. Lal Singh attached the bits with string when they came within sight of the school. The enormous building loomed against the eastern horizon, a black shape against the dark night sky, with lights in the windows like sinister eyes watching them.

Lal Singh instructed the boy. "Young Rab, we must move to a place from which direction the wind is blowing. I will anchor your rope to my leather belt. You will ascend with the kite, letting out the rope as you climb skyward. I will advance most carefully toward the school as you are lifting upward. When we are close enough to the walls you will be looking into windows in order to detect Miss Emmaline's present whereabouts. Please attract her attention without setting off the doubtless unfriendly school personages and any prowling minions. Assure her of our helpful intents. Once you have done this, we will retire quietly for your descending purposes."

Rab nodded. It was the most he'd ever heard Lal Singh say. He did have one concern.

"Lal Singh, it isn't decent for a lad to peer in lassies' windows at night. There were a bloke in Upper Owlthwaite 'oo did that and he got thrown in jail to protect 'im from the lassies and their mams."

Lal Singh looked very seriously at Rubberbones. "That is an excellent point for you to be making. This man of whom you speak was clearly a reprobate character and deserving of chastisement, possibly beatings with leather shoes. You must approach each window with modesty uppermost in your mind, possibly shutting the eyes if necessary, though not to the extent of failing to spot Miss Emmaline. Remember, we perform this task for a purpose, and you must risk the unpleasant possibilities of perhaps seeing young ladies in their informalities and unmentionabilities. I am sure that no god will strike you dead in this matter."

Rab smiled nervously. If only Aunt Lucy could do this part. But he quickly put aside this idea. For though he was a shy and modest boy, Rab was a loyal and brave one as well.

He felt the wind blow through him as he clasped the framework of the big paper kite. Rope trailed from his harness to Lal Singh's heavy military belt. As the breeze lifted the wing, he kicked off from a flat rock that stood out on the moor. Within moments, Rubberbones was rising.

CHAPTER 11

A Tap at the Window

Emmaline was not happy. Somehow the story of her tripping up Josie had spread around the school in a matter of hours and developed into several interesting, sensational and wildly untrue versions, most of which contradicted one another.

"Emmaline attacked Josie with a stick for no reason."

"Josie's going to kill Emmaline now. Or at least maim her for life."

"Emmaline went on a rampage with a hockey stick."

"No, it was an ax, painted to look like a hockey stick."

"It was that Charlotte girl. Emmaline was going to chop her up with an ax, but Josie stopped her by diving in front of her."

"Gwendolyn and Josie stopped Emmaline from slicing poor Charlotte to pieces with a giant woodcutter's ax."

"Emmaline's a mad ax murderer. That's why she was sent here. She's an orphan who chopped up her parents in —"

"Africa, after a witch doctor put a curse on her — "

That strange thing known as "gossip" was something that Emmaline had always avoided in the past. It didn't interest her. She had better things to think about. But, of course, it meant that Emmaline had no idea how to respond to the rumors about her.

Emmaline sat alone during dinner. She sat alone when all the girls of the Upper Middle gathered around the table and did their homework for the following day. She sat alone in the dormitory after her bath. The other girls were huddled at the far end of the room, but she was in no mood to join them. Amelia would be there, probably smirking her way through an account of how her friend Gwendolyn had hurled herself forward to save Josie, Charlotte and fifteen other girls from a raging Emmaline with her hockey stick whirling above her head like a huge executioner's ax, screaming, "DIE, INNOCENT BRITISH SCHOOLGIRLS, FOR MY EVIL ONE-EYED GODDESS OF BLOOD DEMANDS SACRIFICE!!!"

Well, perhaps not. Still, Emmaline didn't want to be with them. She took a book and a candle, and went out onto the landing. There was a seat by a window. She could overhear Hannah behind the dormitory door telling a spooky story.

Rubberbones was floating fifty feet above the ground. This didn't bother him at all. What bothered him was that it was dark, and the lamps in the tower windows only made the bare stone walls seem even darker outside the circles of light. Every so often he banged into a wall with a worrying scrape of rock against the paper kite. Rubberbones wasn't sure how much damage his kite could sustain. The kite obeyed the wind much more than it obeyed its pilot — no matter what the boy did to guide it.

The wind was rising in power, and though Lal Singh had the rope attached to his belt, Rab knew that the blowing gusts could lift them both into the cold and stormy North Sea a few hundred feet away.

The other problem was that Rab closed his eyes every time he came near a window, in case he saw anything he wasn't supposed to see. There are boys who would be very willing indeed to look through girls' windows, but Rab was not one of them. Whenever he came up to a window, he tapped, squeezed his eyes shut and counted to ten (so that any young lady who needed to pull on a dressing gown had time to do so). Only then did he peer in through the pane. All of this was guaranteed to cause him tremendous trouble.

It was also guaranteed to attract attention as soon as he reached a lighted window.

———————

As usual, the girls of the Remove were giggling among themselves rather than doing their homework. They expected Matron to march down the hallway to scold them into bed. What they didn't expect was a tap on the window, followed by a small, round face with its eyes scrunched shut and its nose flattened against the glass. The girls shrieked like twelve-year-old banshees.

———————

Miss Silverspoon, the teacher of ladies' etiquette and domestic arts, was in her own room, engrossed with a piece of needlework. It was an ambitious project involving a heavenly cloud on which St. Peter, the Virgin Mary and the queen's late husband, Prince Albert, were all welcoming Miss Silverspoon's recently deceased uncle Silas on his arrival at the Pearly Gates. Just as she sewed the first stitches of her late uncle's bushy eyebrows, she heard a tap on the window, followed by the sight of a small, round face with its eyes scrunched shut and its nose flattened against the glass. Miss Silverspoon thought she recognized the face. "Uncle Silas! Back from the dead!" she wailed. "Back from the dead — to see my embroidery!"

———————

Josie was alone in the games equipment room, taping her hockey stick. She did this every night because, to her, a properly taped hockey stick was always a thing of beauty. (She'd once stitched that phrase on a sampler in Miss Silverspoon's class.)

Like the others, Josie was not expecting a tap on the window, followed by a small, round face with its eyes scrunched shut and its nose flattened against the glass. But she didn't shriek. And she did not wail. Instead she stood up, made her most menacing face and smacked the window with her stick.

———

Emmaline heard the shriek. Then she heard the wail. At first she thought that it was her classmates, for Hannah's story had to be reaching its climax of horror by now. Then she heard the crash of glass.

Hannah was a wonderful teller of terrifying tales — but surely she couldn't cause glass to break?

At that moment, Emmaline heard something else. A tap on the window, followed by a small, round face with its eyes scrunched shut and its nose flattened against the glass.

Emmaline knew that squashed nose. Leaning forward, she opened the window latch.

"Aaaaagghhhh!!!!!" cried Rubberbones.

"Hello, Rab," said Emmaline, as if this were all quite normal. "You've got glass in your hair."

"Miss Em! Aye! There's a monster in one of the windows below!"

Emmaline took a deep breath. The important thing was that Rubberbones was safely perched in the window with a kite billowing behind him in the wind. Monsters were a minor issue at the moment. "What are you doing here?"

"I wanted to find out how you are. Yer aunt's come to get you out, if she can. She's going to see the headmistress in t'morning. But if that doesn't work, we'll 'ave to rescue you!"

"Rescue me? That's wonderful! But how?"

"Er, dunno right off. Miss Aunt Lucy and Lal Singh will come up wi' something good. Can you be 'ere at this window same time tomorrow night? I'll come and let you know all about it then."

There was commotion coming down the corridor. The voices of Miss Scantcommon and Miss Sharpelbow were raised. The shrieking of the Removes had spread to the younger girls, the Shells. Miss Silverspoon's wailing had not faded away, but seemed to echo off the very walls of the tower. It all seemed to be heading this way. Emmaline thought it would be a good time to close the window and sit quietly with her schoolbooks.

"Tomorrow, then," she whispered, turning back toward the window. But Rubberbones had gone. As she fixed the latch, she could see a shadowy blur fleeting across the sky. Was it Rubberbones? Or something else?

CHAPTER 12

Sneaking About in the Dead of Day

Morning assembly was a daily ritual at St. Grimelda's. The oak-paneled hall known as "Big School" was filled with benches where the girls sat in ranks, youngest at the front. There were a few hymns, sung largely off-key, accompanied by an organ wheezing like an old man who has walked too far uphill. One of the teachers would read a text from the Old Testament, chosen to emphasize the risks in offending the Almighty. The reader always announced these like punishment lists. Emmaline thought to herself that St. Grimelda's promoted a fierce, bad-tempered God, rather like Mrs. Wackett, but a bit farther away. Mrs. Wackett herself was the headlining top-o'-the-bill at assembly. It was her chance to inject staff and pupils with a good dose of fear early in the day that would last well into the afternoon.

And, after the uproar of last night, she ought to be in top, roaring form.

As it turned out, she was exactly the opposite. She was calm. Strangely so, thought Emmaline. When Mrs. Wackett was trying to be sweet, it was ... unnatural. What was it all about?

"Gels, you may have noticed a certain amount of, erm, excitement in the dormitories last night. Quite normal for young gels to tell ghost stories and see things that aren't there. A window was accidentally broken in the, ah, excitement — simply the natural exuberance of young people! So, just remember in future to try and keep those high spirits in check — and don't believe in things that don't exist! There are no goblins or trolls at St. Grimelda's!"

"Witches, though," thought Emmaline to herself. It was very, very odd. The Wicked Wackett had almost smiled at the whole assembly. That couldn't be good, could it?

Rubberbones stood alone on the moors, watching St. Grimelda's from a distance. It was mid-morning, with the wind of the previous evening still blowing fresh. He shook his head in disgust when he thought about last night's strange ascent up the walls of the dormitory tower. He was angry at himself for bungling the whole thing, trying to peer inside while attempting — at the very same time — to keep his eyes shut for the sake of decency. It couldn't be done. He'd been angry at that lunatic girl who'd come at him with the hockey stick (though he could see her point of view). No, it was his own fault, because he'd thought she was some kind of monster when really she was just a big girl with a homely face. That didn't make her an ogre, nor the fact that she'd smashed a window, spraying glass all over him, and poked him with a big piece of wood. It had frightened the living daylights out of him, and he'd been a babbling idiot after that. It was dead lucky he'd found Miss Em at all, given how he'd messed up the whole thing.

He smacked his head. What a bungler, to be sure!

The kite had survived, which was the main thing. He'd have it ready for this evening, just in case they needed it. He'd find out when Miss Aunt Lucy came back from the school. Lal Singh had driven her up there an hour ago. Rab had strict instructions to stay hidden on the moors and watch the school gates for anything unusual that might happen. He had crouched down in a clump of bracken for a while until he got bored, then tramped about in the long grass, crouching occasionally in case somebody might be watching from the school towers. That didn't make much sense, of course, because anyone who looked would have seen a small figure bobbing about for no obvious reason. But Rubberbones, as we already know, was a man of action, and men of action don't always think things through very clearly. He was simply killing time until the dogcart came back. Hoping Miss Em would be in it.

———

Emmaline knew that something strange was going on. Even if nothing had happened the night before, she'd have guessed that this was no normal day. And, since she was no normal girl, she decided to watch for interesting developments.

In other words, she was going to snoop.

Emmaline had told Hannah about Rubberbones and the kite and asked her to stage a diversion in class. Hannah willingly agreed, but when she carried it out, Emmaline considered her scheme a low trick. Hannah could have pretended to faint, or have a coughing fit, but instead she tripped the incomprehensible foreign princess while practicing an elaborate curtsy (the kind one might use at a palace garden party when meeting the Prince of Wales, for example). Hannah stuck her toe out, sending Purnah staggering. Somehow the princess's arm caught Hannah by the leg and sent the girl crashing into Miss Silverspoon's tapestry. This caused the teacher of etiquette and domestic arts to shriek hysterically, setting off several of the girls, some of them just for the fun of it. Jane and Margaret cried because they always did. Princess Purnah looked surprised and apologized loudly in her own language, uttering the strange phrase "Trikk! Porok! Glekk!" as she stamped on Hannah's wrist, twice, while helping the groaning girl to her feet.

It was easy for Emmaline to drop a pencil, crawl across the floor to where it had fallen right outside the doorway and make a quiet escape.

Emmaline tiptoed down the corridor. There was a window at the end that overlooked the quadrangle. She peered out. Her instincts were good. Below stood Aunt Lucy's dogcart, and next to it was Lal Singh. The Sikh's eyes scanned the courtyard as he petted Earnest's ears. Emmaline's first instinct was to call out. But everyone would hear, which would not help at all. She could see the caretaker staring suspiciously at Lal Singh from his post in the gatehouse. He was the kind of man who always suspected something was going on, even when it wasn't. She'd have to sneak all the way down the stairs and across the quad under Pinchbeak's nose to reach Lal Singh. That wasn't going to be easy. She had fifteen minutes before the bell brought girls pouring out of class.

Emmaline tiptoed down the stairs. She slipped through an archway, hung with portraits of fierce headmistresses from long ago, along a shadowed portico and straight into Josie Pinner, coming the other way.

"Oof!" said both girls together. Emmaline meant it more, though, since Josie was twice her size. She looked up at the girl she had deliberately tripped on the ball court so recently. Josie glowered down at her.

"You aren't supposed to be here, are you?"

Emmaline might have said that she was running a message for a teacher, but lying did not come easily to her. "Er, not really."

"Well, duck back behind that bench over there. Wackett's in a rare temper today. I just got yelled at for breaking a window, and she's frothing at the lips because some girl's auntie wants to visit without an appointment. I heard her tell Matron."

"Thanks," said Emmaline. She was surprised at Josie's friendliness.

"Only fair, I say. You stopped me crushing two girls yesterday. I never even saw 'em in front of me. Would've been a nasty crock-up for them, and I'd never have known 'til it was done. So I owe you one!"

With that, the big girl was off. Moments later, Emmaline heard the voices of Mrs. Wackett and Miss Scantcommon coming down the stairs. She ducked behind the bench that Josie had recommended. This was lucky, because both women stopped right in front of her. They were looking out of a window to the quad below.

"Who does that woman think she is, coming in here demanding to see a gel? Not even a parent, merely an aunt!" It was Mrs. Wackett speaking.

"I hope you told her she couldn't see the child?" said Matron.

"Oh, I sent her away with a flea in her ear, I can tell you. It's one of those infuriating days. First of all, the little girls are squealing like banshees, then that oaf Josie Pinner is smashing things, Miss Silverspoon's in hysterics and everyone's seeing a face at the window."

"You spoke to the Pinner girl, then?"

"Indeed I did, Ethelswitha. She's not telling the truth, I can say that for certain. She claims that she swung her hockey

stick for no apparent reason and then accidentally let it slip through her fingers so that it crashed into the window, knocking out three panes. She saw no strange faces, either, which is odd. Everyone else in the school — including those who have no window at all — came face-to-face with a variety of goblins, pixies and flying monkeys last night. Usual childish stupidity, one might suppose, but I suspect that something else is going on."

"And then, this woman today?" said Miss Scantcommon.

"I don't know. Probably no connection with last night, but one can't be too mistrustful. I pride myself on trusting no one. And I am concerned about Josie's lying to us. It doesn't add up. There is something we don't know."

"Do you think we should —"

"Yes, I think we should let our winged friends have a little flutter this evening."

Emmaline shivered and shrank as small as she could into the space behind the bench. The two women marched off along the hallway, their footsteps clicking in unison, like guardsmen on parade.

Emmaline moved quickly yet silently toward the window. She could see the quad, the gatehouse, the back of Pinchbeak's head. But Lal Singh and the dog cart were gone.

———

Rubberbones was still hopping about on the moor when the dogcart emerged from the gateway of St. Grimelda's. His heart was in his mouth, hoping to see Emmaline sitting on the high seat. His spirits fell when he saw only Lal Singh and Aunt Lucy. They fell farther when he saw the kindly woman's expression.

He knew then that he was going to have to rescue Emmaline.

Rescuing young ladies from locked stone towers is a difficult business. But that was no obstacle for a twelve-year-old boy who could fly. Sort of, anyway.

CHAPTER 13

Creatures of the Night

It was clear to Emmaline that this moment — now — was a time for action. Rubberbones had come to her window, by kite, and told her that he'd be back. Aunt Lucy had come to the school and been refused when she asked to see her. Mrs. Wackett and Miss Scantcommon were behaving suspiciously. Altogether, it was no time to put on bedroom slippers and settle down with a nice cup of cocoa.

It was a time for gathering her valuables and putting on sensible shoes and the kind of clothes you might wear for a long walk across the moors, or for committing a burglary.

Since St. Grimelda's had forbidden her to bring anything she might consider valuable, that was a short list. And since the school insisted that its pupils wear a cheerful mix of black and dark gray, these deep shades aided secret activities after dark. The only real issue was suitable clothes, for the usual daily dress of long skirts and vast amounts of underwear (normal for all Victorian females) was not what you'd want for anything even remotely active. Emmaline decided her gym clothes would have to do.

For one final detail Emmaline requested Hannah's help once more.

"Can you arrange another diversion for me this evening? About eight o'clock?" Emmaline asked her friend.

"You mean, keep all the other girls occupied while your boy appears at the window?"

"Exactly. Tell them another of your stories. A really scary one."

"While your sweetheart comes to your rescue! How romantic!" sniffed Hannah. Prince Charming, in her tales, was not a grubby, freckled twelve-year-old boy who appeared to be frightened out of his wits.

"He's not my sweetheart. He's twelve. He's like a little brother."

"But he flies, you say?"

"Well, he bounces when he falls, and he can hang on to kites and he piloted the flying machine I designed and built," Emmaline explained.

Hannah sniffed again. "And you say that I make up outrageous stories!"

She flounced off before Emmaline could reply.

"That horrible woman barely gave me time to remove my hat. In fact, I didn't remove my hat."

Aunt Lucy was clearly furious. She threw her hat onto the floor of the inn and jumped on it, flattening it, and kicked it into a corner.

"Said I couldn't see Emmaline under any circumstances. That I wasn't her parent, that I wasn't paying her school fees, that —"

"It would be better if you did not destroy your admirable headgear, memsahib," suggested Lal Singh reasonably.

Aunt Lucy had, indeed, ripped a long gash in the hat's crown. "Well, it was really what I expected all along. I'd have been shocked if the wretched hag had let me visit Emmaline. Did you manage what you went for?"

The tall Indian gracefully poured another cup of tea. "I was able to identify the window most clearly in daylight. Unfortunately, the tower is too far from the outside wall to be trying any kind of ladder. She would have to be climbing from ledge to ledge to reach a suitable spot to descend with ropes, and I am doubting that Miss Emmaline, though an estimable young lady in all ways, has sufficient mountaineering accomplishments for such a task."

Aunt Lucy's brow furrowed. "I see. Do you have any suggestions as to how we should free my niece from the clutches of that harpie and her minions?"

Rubberbones, who had been listening in silence, made a mental note to use the word "minions" in conversation. He didn't really know what it meant, but it sounded good.

"I regret it, but, since we have no dynamite, and we cannot wait until Miss Emmaline is reaching the age of eighteen, I believe that we will once again be calling upon young Mr. Burns to elevate his kite."

"So Rab will ascend to Emmaline's window and have her hold on to the kite while you bring it down? Is the kite strong enough for both of them?" asked Aunt Lucy.

"I believe that if we are working on adding an extra wing today, the kite will be strong enough. Miss Emmaline is not a heavy young lady, being long and thinnish," replied Lal Singh.

Rubberbones spoke for the first time. "Ye canna do that," he said, sounding oddly Scottish. "Miss Em is terrified to fly. That's my job. She stays on the ground."

Aunt Lucy looked sternly at the lad. "Robert, Emmaline may be scared, but she's going to have to do it anyway. It's only for a brief drop to the ground, a few moments in the air. She can keep her eyes closed. You must reassure her — tell her it will be all right. And grab on tightly."

Rubberbones shook his head and muttered to himself. Miss Em would be terrified. Still, he couldn't think of another way around it.

———

Emmaline was as ready as she could be. She couldn't think of anything she wanted to take with her. She was dressed in her black games outfit. Tonight, she was going to be rescued.

Emmaline didn't want to think of exactly how this was going to happen. It might involve Lal Singh bursting through the gates on horseback with a chestnut mare for her to leap on and ride away. This seemed unlikely, though, as she was a clumsy rider and would be better on a donkey than a spirited horse. Aunt Lucy might appear with a magistrate's order and a party of police constables. Again, this seemed unlikely. Emmaline was at St. Grimelda's because her mother had paid the fees. Aunt Lucy probably couldn't convince any judge that this old-fashioned girls' school was really a vile prison. Maybe an old hermit woman would emerge from a cave under the school cellars and show her out through ancient tunnels leading to the cliffs below. Maybe ...

But she knew that it would be Rubberbones with his kite, and she'd be terrified and might even fall. Emmaline shuddered.

Dinner was past, homework was done (she hadn't really bothered with hers, as you can imagine) and the Upper Middles were gathered in the common area around Hannah, who was telling one of her most gripping tales.

It had to be almost time —

She suddenly heard a strange noise out there in the night, a sort of high-pitched shriek, like a bird but not like a bird, and a distant, beating sound.

The moor was in full, stumbling darkness. The moon was not up yet, and the path had been slow going for Ernest, who was a very old horse. Aunt Lucy sat silently, her baggage taken from the hotel in readiness for what might be called "a getaway" by someone who read cowboy yarns (which Aunt Lucy sometimes did, aloud, in a bad Texas accent).

The wind was about the same as last night, which was perfect: enough to keep the kite aloft, not enough to make it impossible to steer. Rab was confident about his ability to direct the kite where he wanted, more or less, by lifting one wing or the other or dipping it downward or to the side. He was getting quite good — far better than he had been with the proper flying machines. Really, he'd just sat in those and gone wherever they did.

Lal Singh stopped the cart a good distance away from the school and turned down the lamp. "No good being seen," he explained. He and Rubberbones hoisted the kite from the cart. It was a little heavier than last night because of the extra sail made from canvas stitched over a wooden frame. They pressed ahead, leaving Aunt Lucy (who was not a person who should climb a hill in the dark, carrying a lumbering great kite on her back) in charge of Ernest and the cart.

Rubberbones wasn't normally the sort who imagined things. Imaginative boys don't believe they can fall from great heights without getting hurt. Imaginative boys think of bad things that might happen. Rubberbones never did. He'd even more or less forgotten about the ogre. He knew it was just a mickle great girl.

So when he heard the flapping sound and the shrill calls of something far above him, he thought, "Ey-oop. There's big seagulls out tonight."

He jumped from the same rock as before, the rope snaking beneath him from Lal Singh's belt, and floated up into the night.

Rubberbones's eyes were on the lit window he'd visited the previous evening; it seemed even brighter tonight. Emmaline must have put a lamp right behind the glass. He was above the outer wall, looking up at the tower. The window was perhaps twenty feet above him.

He was rising gently when he heard the sound again.

Big seagulls.

Now there was flapping over his head. The birds had to be circling. Rubberbones looked up, seeing nothing but the big new wing of the kite. Suddenly there was a howling shriek, and two vicious talons stabbed into the canvas, ripping the fabric. The wing buckled but did not break away. Rubberbones was jarred as the impact knocked the kite sideways, spinning crazily off course. He clutched the frame, his knuckles whitening on the wood. He swiveled his head to see what had happened. The flapping sound seemed more distant, and a shape — a monstrous shape — covered the sliver of moon that had begun to rise. It was the silhouette of a great bird, a predator on the hunt. There was something uncanny about it. It shrieked in short barks as it circled.

It was talking to its mate.

The second creature came in beneath the kite. Rab barely saw the gaping beak, with razor-sharp teeth snapping, as the beast rose to the attack. The boy kicked at it, catching a boot against its scaly topside somewhere behind the head. It was like no bird he had ever seen. Instead of feathers, it had dry, mottled, leathery-looking skin. The head was like a falcon's, but longer and weirdly reptilian. The monster (and this was no large girl with a grim expression and a hockey stick) was bigger than —

Well, a twelve-year-old boy.

CHAPTER 14

The Dangers of Broken Furniture

Emmaline sensed that something was horribly wrong. She was at the window, staring into the darkness. The lamp she had placed next to the glass made the night outside even blacker. There was noise out there: strange sounds she didn't recognize. Weird, screeching calls and the flapping of something in the wind. But there was no sign of Rubberbones. She could see down into the dark well of the quad and the inner lights of the gatehouse and Pinchbeak's cabin. Beyond that, nothing. There were a few stars, but not enough to bring any real light into the sky. The moon was not visible from this window; if it had already risen, it was hiding behind the tower and was certainly not shining brightly.

Something suddenly flashed by the window. Emmaline took a step backward. What in the world was that?

She did not think it was a big seagull.

There was more shrieking outside. Stepping back to the window, Emmaline saw the kite. It was twisting like a mad thing, with a small figure — Rubberbones, surely — kicking out against some dark shape below him. Another shape was draped above the top wing of the kite. Suddenly the top wing was wrenched away. The kite began to spin downward until it disappeared from view.

There was a crash below.

Rubberbones hit the tiled roof hard, rolling over. As always, the impact simply caused him to bounce upright. The damaged frame draping his shoulders fell to his feet. He looked about, eyes round with fear.

"What the flippin' 'eck were that?" he asked aloud. He'd been mauled by village boys and farmers' dogs and once by an unhappy pig, but none of them were monsters. Tonight he'd been attacked by something unearthly: hideous scaly birds with wingspans like sails and teeth like razors. He grasped the kite as if it were some kind of shield, in case the creatures came shrieking down at him. Instinctively, he backed up, to where the roof he stood on met the wall of the tower, and flattened himself against the stone. He breathed carefully, not moving.

Nothing happened.

He'd swear the winged creatures were gone. Rab looked up to see the light burning in Emmaline's window. It wasn't all that far if he was careful with the handholds. He placed the kite in the shadow of the wall. It was ripped badly, and the whole new upper wing had gone, fallen who-knows-where. The main supporting struts of the frame seemed to be in place, but this was no time to be examining it. He'd have to leave it, though he undid the rope and tied it twice around his middle. Lal Singh was still tied to the other end, but there was no way to contact him. "He must be worried sick," thought Rubberbones. "Still, nowt t'be done about that." Nowt — nothing — indeed.

The stones of the tower were quite roughly hewn, allowing him to shinny his way up the wall. Rab knew not to look down. If the leathery birds got at him, well, he'd kick 'em again. So he told himself, anyway, for bravery is always easier said than done. He worked his way slowly, and at last pulled his chest over the window ledge with a groan. It wasn't as easy as Farmer Jenks's orchard wall.

As she saw the pale cheeks and huge eyes suddenly appear out of the darkness, Emmaline gave a start, then breathed a huge sigh of relief. She flung open the window, almost knocking the boy completely off the ledge.

Fortunately, he pulled himself up into the window space. He was wild-eyed and incoherent. "Blabbering," his gran would have called it.

"Miss Em! Kite's broke! On the roof down there. Big birds! Flippin' great beasts they was! 'Orrible things! Quick! Here's a bit o' rope!"

Rab untied the frayed end of his rope from around his middle and shoved it into her hands. This was his escape plan? Emmaline frowned. "What, Rab?"

"Tie it to summat strong and we'll slide down it!"

That was easier said than done since the school was not built with convenient iron rings for escaping. There was a heavy desk that might do the trick. The beastly old thing groaned as they pushed it across the floor to the window. Rab quickly lashed the rope around one of its legs.

"Rab, what's at the other end of the rope?"

"Oh, it's tied to Lal Singh's waist. Come on, then!"

Emmaline looked out of the open window. The rope disappeared into darkness, sloping gradually downward. Was it snagged on the battlements of the outer wall? Was Lal Singh outside the wall, or had he somehow got into the quad? How strong was Lal Singh? How strong was the rope?

Emmaline thought about things far too much, which was her problem. Rubberbones thought about things far too little, and that was his.

"Follow me, and we'll be off, then!" Rab clambered, monkeylike, out of the window. He was hanging, face upward, with hands leading and feet crossed over the rope, like a moving hammock. He really was like some form of cheerful Yorkshire ape, thought Emmaline.

"But I can't do that!" she whispered.

Emmaline was holding the rope, peering out, when she heard a girlish voice behind her.

"Aha! Caught you in the act!"

Amelia stood in the doorway, hands on her hips and a smirk on her face. Gwendolyn was at her side, scowling. Other girls were behind them — Petunia and Petronella twittering, Jane and Margaret crying, Anna silent, Bernadette staring, Mary-Alice giggling, Princess Purnah looking on with an excited grin. Hannah was at the very back, her eyes full of sadness.

The familiar, hard footsteps of Miss Scantcommon came ringing down the stairs.

Emmaline let go of the rope. There was a sharp tug at the other end, and the leg of the old desk that Rab had lashed the rope onto came away with a horrible rending sound. The desk crashed onto the floor with an almighty clatter. The broken leg was whipped away by the rope and sailed right out the open window.

"As though things weren't going badly enough," thought Emmaline.

If Emmaline's caution was her undoing, Rubberbones's urge to take any wild risk at all almost led to disaster. He knew that Lal Singh was at the other end of the rope, but he had no idea what lay between. He had no idea whether the leathery birds were still flying. As a matter of fact, he had forgotten them completely; that was fifteen minutes ago, and fifteen minutes was a long time when Rubberbones was excited. What was bothering him right now were three things:

First, Miss Em was not following behind him, and it was very hard to climb back and see where she was. He was sliding along the taut rope.

Second, the rope burned his hands the faster he went, and

he was sliding fast. If he had any skin left on his palms, it was only because they were tough to begin with.

Third, the rope did not lead straight down toward Lal Singh. It was caught on one of the battlements of the school wall. Rubberbones found this out when —

THUMP! He crashed into a solid stone barrier that had been doing a sound job of keeping people both in and out since knights were bold and walls were thick.

As he smashed into the wall, the jolt broke his grip on the rope, flipped him into the air and dropped him twenty-five feet onto the hard ground below. Most people wouldn't like that at all, but Rubberbones wasn't worried about a little bit of a fall.

"Lal Singh! Are you there?" he called out. He was sprawled on the ground. Truth to tell, twenty-five feet is a long way to fall. If an ordinary boy did it, he'd be lucky to come out of it alive, or at least without many bones broken. But Rubberbones simply curled into a ball as he dropped, bounced twice in a way that defies all reasonable medical explanation (so don't ask) and rolled over onto his back. He could see a figure. "Lal Singh!"

A man who was perhaps half the height and a bare one-thousandth of the goodness of Lal Singh was standing over Rubberbones. It was the gatekeeper, Pinchbeak. Rab had never met the man, and first impressions were not good.

"What 'ave we 'ere?" sneered the old coot. "An interloper? A burglar?"

He reached out and seized Rubberbones by the ear. He was the kind of man who would always seize you by the ear if he got the chance.

All at once he let go. "Oof!" Pinchbeak fell down in a heap. A desk leg tied to a rope had hit him on the back of the head. Rubberbones didn't think twice about this sudden development. He didn't care how this unpleasant man had

come to be knocked out cold by a flying desk leg. It was something to do with God, he was certain.

He was up and running for the gatehouse. The lamp hanging outside Pinchbeak's cabin showed the little door cut into the gates. It had a latch and a pair of big bolts. The low moaning coming from behind him suggested that the unconscious man was returning to life. Rab thought the gatekeeper was unlikely to appreciate a bump on the noggin, so he quickly slid the bolts, flipped the latch and fled into the night.

CHAPTER 15

The Black Tower

Emmaline stood silently as Miss Scantcommon glared at her with the kind of fury that goes far beyond ordinary anger. All the blood had drained from Matron's face. It was as if something so appalling had happened that she was going to snap. Right now.

Instead, she said, in a voice that was low and soft, "Miss Cayley, you'll be going to the Black Tower."

The Black Tower. The *other* tower, the forbidden tower.

Emmaline followed Miss Scantcommon out of the room, keeping her face as blank as she could. She was determined to hide her frustration and fear. Her classmates, on the other hand, reacted exactly as she'd expected them to.

Margaret and Jane cried. Anna was stonily silent. Mary-Alice chuckled like the mad child she was. Hannah appeared to be trying to hold back tears. Princess Purnah's eyes flashed. Amelia smiled the nastiest smile Emmaline had ever seen. Gwendolyn was at her elbow, scowling. Petunia and Petronella giggled. And Bernadette fainted right away onto the hard-tiled floor.

———

The innkeeper had let them return to their rooms without comment. Money's money, everyone knows that.

Rubberbones was depressed, thinking about how close he'd been to rescuing Emmaline. Aunt Lucy was depressed as she brought in three cups of cocoa: ordinary, boring cocoa from the hotel kitchen, with no mugwort or mistletoe to liven up the taste.

"If she'd just followed me down the rope —" began the boy.

"You'd have both ended up on the ground!" replied Aunt Lucy. "The rope was not made to carry people like that. You'd be all right, but Emmaline almost certainly would not. She'd have broken —" Aunt Lucy didn't want to think about what she might have broken.

Lal Singh came in from the stable. He, too, looked depressed as he sat down.

"Any ideas on what we can do to get Emmaline out of there?" asked Aunt Lucy.

The room was silent.

Emmaline thought it was definitely a cell. Not a bedroom but a cell. Miss Scantcommon had left her there all night without a lamp or candle, food or water. The door was secured with massive iron locks. The morning light had woken her, streaming in from the narrow window high above the bed. That and the fact that she was shivering. She was able to stand on her hard, single bunk and pull herself up by the bars to have a look outside (Miss Sharpelbow's savage gym classes had been some help to her). There was no glass in the window frame. No wonder she was cold.

The sun was rising. As far as she could see, the cold, churning waters of the North Sea washed into the shore. Emmaline pulled herself even higher to get a vantage point, and realized that she was looking down, vertically, a hundred feet or more. Her cell was on the eastern face of the Black Tower, built flush with the rock face of the cliffs above the sea.

As cells go, this didn't seem like a bad one. There were no skeletons hanging in chains or rats scurrying about. The walls were even feebly whitewashed. As Emmaline looked at the walls more carefully, ancient graffiti could be seen.

The whitewash was meant to cover it. She could make out names and initials: "Bunty Bagshot 1765" and "F.D.T. 12-11-1804." She was not the first girl sent up here, by any means.

The door opened, bolts grating as they slid back. It was Matron, the always charmless Miss Scantcommon.

"Come on, Miss Cayley. We are going to see Mrs. Wackett. You have some explaining to do."

Miss Scantcommon led Emmaline into Mrs. Wackett's office. The headmistress, vast and bloated like a huge toad, was awaiting her. She was almost bubbling with rage. Emmaline stood before her desk, hands crossed in front of her. "Look obedient," she thought. "Say as little as possible." No point in arguing with an enraged monster.

"Miss Cayley! You were caught last night, leaning out of an open window with a rope in your hands. A few moments later, Mr. Pinchbeak had an encounter with a small person who assaulted him with vicious blows to the head and ran away. Pinchbeak found that same rope on the ground this morning with the remains of a valuable piece of school property attached to it. Would you like to explain what was going on?"

Emmaline did not feel like explaining anything. She would have liked to be somewhere else, but of course she wasn't.

Mrs. Wackett took Emmaline's silence as a reason to go on. She came out from behind her desk to display her terrible bulk.

"Two nights ago there was an uproar in which a number of staff and pupils saw something or someone outside. A window was broken. There was a great deal of foolishness about the identity of this person; the excitable ones thought it was a vampire or some such nonsense, but I think we can be sure it was your visitor. Then yesterday your silly aunt foolishly decided to come and see me without an appointment. She demanded that she be allowed to see you. I refused, of course, and turned her away. And then, last night — well, it seems clear that there was some form of idiotic plan for you to abscond from the school. Do you have anything to say for yourself?"

Emmaline did not. She had decided to stay silent, no matter what. She tried to think of flying machines and earthworm sandwiches.

Mrs. Wackett leaned forward, her face no more than a few inches from Emmaline's. It was horrific sheer ferocity and lizardly breath mixed with sickly lilac perfume. Emmaline flinched.

"You can play that game, my gel, but you will not like the consequences, I can promise you. I have spoken to your little friend Hannah. She isn't as disobedient as you when it comes to answering questions. She told me all about your sneaking around the school while she kept everyone else busy. You must realize that here at St. Grimelda's we have ways of finding out the truth."

Emmaline felt stunned at Hannah's betrayal. She said nothing, but her fingers formed into tight fists. *How could she?*

"Tougher than your little chum, then?" snarled Mrs. Wackett. "We'll see what you are made of. You can clean up after the birds in the tower. No — you can *feed* them their supper!" She smiled the most hostile smile Emmaline had ever seen.

And with that vile, though very strange, threat, Emmaline was whisked away by the strong hand of Miss Scantcommon. Back to the Black Tower.

As they began to cross the quad, the bell rang to change classes and girls poured out of doorways at a rush. As soon as they saw Emmaline and Matron together, and where it was they were going, all heads turned away.

An hour after sunrise, Rubberbones was back among the rocks on the high moor, watching the school. He had left his bed before Lal Singh awoke and crept up the mile or so in the last darkness of the night.

Perhaps he'd see something. Think of something.

Nothing.

CHAPTER 16

Things That Shouldn't Be

Miss Scantcommon led Emmaline up a flight of winding steps to a chamber. It had huge plank doors with iron bands, uneven flagstones and an ancient smell of something horrible. The circular room took up the whole floor space of the Black Tower. Another staircase stood against the wall, leading upward through a trapdoor in the roof. A grille of iron bars divided the room in half. There was a barred metal door at one end. On the other side of the bars huge, blackened timbers like ships' masts seemed to grow from the stone floor. It was a monstrous perch of some kind. Above it, in the ceiling, was an iron grate fixed to a hinge mechanism. Something like a machine, but from the days before modern engineering. "Odd," thought Emmaline.

The floor was filthy. It was littered with meat scraps and bones and what appeared to be the biggest, most unpleasant bird droppings ever seen. Or smelled. She stepped back from the repugnant mess.

"Here's one bucket. One shovel. One broom," said Matron. "I shall return in one hour. I expect the place to be spotless." She didn't seem concerned about the appalling stench in the room, but then again, she was leaving.

Emmaline was screwing up her nerve to begin her hideous task when the door clanged open.

"Hello again," said a voice from behind her.

Emmaline jumped.

It was Josie Pinner.

"Sorry 'bout that. This is your first time cleaning out the

birds, is it? I remember mine. Scared me to death at the time. Look at the mess they leave."

"What are you here for?" asked Emmaline.

"Breaking a window with my hockey stick. Twice in two days. Different windows, of course."

"That's not fair at all!" exclaimed Emmaline. "They were just accidents, weren't they?"

"So I told Wackett. I play dumb when it suits me. I actually busted 'em both on purpose."

"But why?"

"First time, which was the night before last, I thought it were a peeper. I was upstairs where we keep the games kit. Some bloke from the village with a few drinks inside him. So I shoved the stick through the window. Smashed the glass all over his face — made him clear off sharpish! Then last night, they had the birds flying; one was hovering outside my dorm window. I thought, 'Right, then, I'll give you what for.' I hate 'em, you know. Nasty, vile creatures. So I did the same thing and caught him behind the head with my stick. Oh, the way he jumped! Took off like the devil was after him. Whatever it was he was hunting got a gift from me, all right, 'cos the bird lost all interest in his dinner from that moment on!" Josie chuckled, and Emmaline joined in.

Emmaline was beginning to really like Josie. She was brave and she was honest. She didn't speak like most of the other girls with their affected "posh" accents. She was down-to-earth. And she didn't seem to care what people thought, either.

"I think that the peeper and the thing the bird was chasing were one and the same," said Emmaline. "It was my friend Rab — I call him Rubberbones, everyone does — trying to rescue me. He can fly, sort of, with a kite. Or he could, until last night."

"Ah," said Josie. "I 'spect I must've scared him."

As the two girls got down to the filthy business of shoveling up bones and scraps and dung, Emmaline told Josie the whole story. It took a while, but the chore was not a quick task; evidently, cleaning out the birds was not a daily duty for anyone. This kind of nastiness was the product of weeks or months.

"So the last I saw of Rab he was swinging out of the window on a rope. The kite had been smashed up — probably by the birds — and he wanted me to follow him. Then I got caught trying to escape, and the table we'd tied the rope to broke and I think Rab must have had an accident himself. I don't know what happened to him. I just hope he's all right."

———

Rubberbones stood on the rock. He'd been there for ages, looking at the school. He still had no ideas that seemed helpful.

Someone placed a hand on Rab's shoulder.

"Your people will wonder where you are, my lad," said the Gypsy chief, also known as Sid. "And you cannot free your friend by standing in the wind, freezing like this."

"I don't know what to do," said Rab forlornly.

"I don't either, right now at this moment. I shall ask some of my traveling fellows for advice. Many of my people have needed to be rescued from bad things and bad places over the years. It takes patience and planning. Sometimes it is necessary to find a friend to help you out." Then his voice changed to a more familiar tone. "Right now, you look like you might benefit from a nice cuppa tea."

The wagon — just the one — was parked behind a rocky ridge a hundred yards away. Madame ZaZa, also known as Norah, had put the kettle on to boil. "Hello, dearie," she said when she saw Rab. "I told Sid here ye'd be needing some help as time went by. I watch you in my crystal ball every now and then, just to keep an eye on things. So, I says to Sid, I says, let's you and me go off and see what we can do to be of assistance. The rest of 'em have taken their wagons down toward Lincoln; we can catch up with 'em later. What's this about big birds and your friend being trapped in a castle, then? It's a rum do and no mistake."

Rubberbones wondered what a "rum do" might be. Perhaps it was a sort of cake. He could always find room for a piece of cake.

———— ⋙◦◦◦⋘ ————

Emmaline heard a slow, creaking noise. The grate in the ceiling was descending. Shrill, piercing noises rent the air, echoing off the chamber walls.

Josie spoke in a whisper in case Miss Scantcommon came in. "That'll be Matron letting the birds down. They've got a coop on the roof, but this is where they sleep and eat. It's not time for either, so she probably just wants to scare us. But I've seen 'em before, and I'm not scared. Funny-looking birds, though. I had a book out of the library about birds of prey — eagles and hawks and that sort of thing. None of them looked like that. The book was only about British and European birds, so perhaps that's it. They might have come from somewhere else."

Another noise, and something dropped heavily onto the giant perch. Emmaline stared. Her face went pale. Her eyes grew big. Her mouth was dry.

The creature behind the iron grille looked at her with cold, golden eyes. It had a grotesque, leathery face that extended into a savage beak. It wrapped its wings, batlike, around itself. The skin was hard, scaly in places, blotchy and more green than yellow. It had no feathers like an ordinary bird, but it did have claws with talons. Huge talons with dagger-sharp ends.

"Josie," said Emmaline very quietly. "I have seen one of these in a book. I think this is what they call a pterodactyl."

"A what?" said Josie.

The pterodactyl hissed.

"Shut up, you nasty beast!" barked Josie. She didn't care what it was.

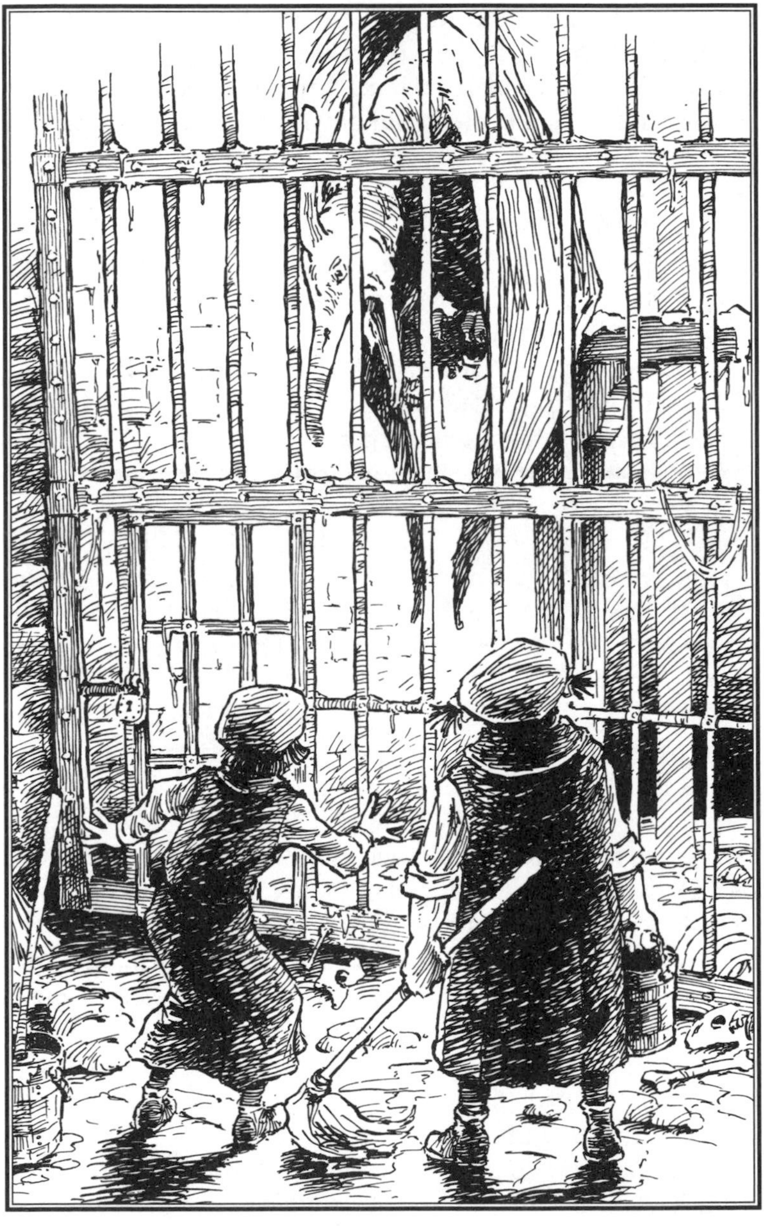

CHAPTER 17

Feeding the Birds

Emmaline was sitting on the hard bed of her cell. It had been a couple of hours since she had come face to face with the pterodactyl. Two of them, actually. The second had come down through the grating as Matron came in to usher the girls back to their cells. She was still struck with fear recalling the icy-cold stare and the saw-toothed, leathery menace of them. She was also thinking furiously.

How was it possible for there to be a pterodactyl here? Here, in a school for girls, in England, in 1894. Because, even though it was a strange school run by cruel and inhuman guardians, it was still not possible to keep pterodactyls. You could keep fierce dogs; a lot of people did. You could keep lions and tigers or monkeys and chimpanzees, if you had the money and knew where to go. She'd heard you could even order an elephant at Harrods, the famous shop in London.

Pterodactyls were different. They were related to dinosaurs. Emmaline had read books about dinosaurs, with illustrations of amazing beasts from long ago. Upright monsters with massive teeth — like the allosaurus and *Tyrannosaurus rex* — that shook the earth when they moved. She tried to remember something about pterodactyls. She recalled that some were quite small while others had wings that spanned fifty feet outstretched.

The thing that she had been sure about was that they had become extinct millions of years ago.

Rubberbones left the Gypsy camp (well, it was just the one wagon) and returned to the village. He slipped back into the servants' hall at the hotel. Aunt Lucy and Lal Singh were seated at the rough table.

"Good morning, Robert! We are working on a plan. We haven't got one yet, but when we do, we can get a message to Emmaline," said Aunt Lucy. "The landlord knows a woman who works in the school kitchen who'll take a note for a reasonable price. We are going to *bribe* her." She seemed quite pleased to be bribing someone. It wasn't something she got to do every day.

Rab told them about the arrival of the Gypsies. They all agreed it was good to have friends.

But they still didn't have a plan.

The sun was going down when Miss Scantcommon came for Emmaline once more. Emmaline had eaten nothing all day and hoped that Matron was bringing her something for dinner. But no luck! There was more in store for Miss Emmaline Cayley. Her grumbling stomach was the last thing to worry about.

Miss Scantcommon marched Emmaline back to the chamber, pushed her in and left, locking the door behind her. Josie was lounging on the bench, apparently unconcerned by her surroundings. "Hello, Emmaline!" she said brightly. Emmaline smiled back. It was absurd to be so cheerful in a place like this, but somehow Josie's courage helped to ease the fears rising within her. Josie seemed to sense Emmaline's terror.

"Don't worry," said Josie, patting the seat beside her. "I've been through this lots of times. About once every term I get in trouble — usually for breaking things, though not usually on purpose. I am a bit clumsy sometimes. They send me to Wackett. She expects me to be terrified of her, but I'm not. My parents were missionaries in Africa. I've seen lions and snakes and worse, so she doesn't bother me. Then she decides to let me have another go with the birds. I s'pose the idea is to scare me, so I'll behave myself. At first I was pretty frightened, especially once when Matron let the birds down while I was still cleaning out. She did that on purpose. But I wasn't putting up with any nonsense; I shoved the broom into the nasty thing's open beak with my left hand and smacked it with the bucket in my right. It let out a squawk and flew back up through the grating in a proper hurry, I can tell you! And since then, I'm not worried about 'em. I'm not sure if they recognize me, but I give 'em a bit of a poke with a broom if they get close, and they soon get the idea!"

Emmaline had a thousand questions running through her mind. But Josic seemed to have no curiosity about the dinosaurs in the tower. They just *were*. What she did have was kindness and a lot of common sense.

"What do you know about these birds, Josie?" asked Emmaline.

"Nothing. They're just here, that's all."

Emmaline had a sudden, unrelated thought. She asked Josie about Hannah.

"You mean, why did your friend give you away?"

"Yes."

"Prob'ly she was scared for herself. Didn't want to be seen as your accomplice. She's not as brave as you. St. Grim's pits all the girls against one another so they don't stand up to Wackett and her lot. I've been here since I was ten. You know how many people I've been able to really trust in that time?"

Emmaline shook her head.

"One, so far," replied Josie. "That's *you*. I've only known you for a little while, but you're different from the others. You don't cave in when you're frightened, and you do the right thing, even when it costs you. That's why you tripped me up that time, when I might've turned around and beaten you silly with my stick. I wouldn't — not deliberately, anyway — but you weren't to know that. Most pupils here would have let me run berserk over those two girls. 'Better them than me' is what they'd say. You're different."

Emmaline thought about this. She didn't believe she was brave. Rubberbones was brave, but then again he couldn't be hurt. Josie was brave, but she was very large and athletic. Would they be just as brave if they were skinny and gawky like her?

Emmaline didn't really have time to think about it, because just then there was a dragging sound outside the door, and Pinchbeak came in with an enormous tub. It smelled unpleasant.

"Right, then, *ladies*" — he said the word with a sneer to make sure they knew he didn't mean it as a compliment — "you may feed our beauties. At your leisure. No 'urry at all."

He cackled as he went out to operate the lever to open the grating. Josie strode over to the tub. "'S all right, really. It's from the local butcher's shop. Just beef hearts and brains and gristle and guts — nothing nasty! And Mr. Pinchbeak has been good enough to let us have a shovel to pass it through the bars. He must be in a good mood!"

Emmaline felt sick. The grating clanged open. There was a rustle of dry, batlike wings and a flurry of screeching as the enormous birds descended. Both pterodactyls were at the bars, beaks snapping. They were making the most tremendous noise, shrieks and almost barks.

Josie smiled. "You want your dinner, then?"

Using the shovel to throw the meat slops into the cage, the two girls fed the birds. Josie finally upended the tub against the bars. The monstrous creatures ate like wild dogs — if dogs could flap about and drop bits of raw flesh from above. It was a hideous thing to behold.

Curiously, at the end of it, Emmaline wasn't nearly as scared as she had been before. Her friend showed no fear of the darting jaws of the pterodactyls. Josie had smacked one with the shovel when it got too close; it had recoiled from her blow, hissing and snapping, but still fell back. Emmaline was impressed.

"They aren't so tough when they're not flying," said Josie, chuckling. "Oh, by the way, I looked out of my cell window after we talked earlier. There was something on the roof, over where the main block meets the tower. It's tucked into a corner, so you prob'ly can't see it from the ground. I saw it this morning, but I didn't realize what it was 'til later. It's your friend's kite. When we have a chance, let's fetch it in and have a look at it."

Yes, it was good to have friends.

CHAPTER 18

A Fearless Schoolgirl, a Crafty Nephew and a Mad Professor

Emmaline was lying in her own bed in the Upper Middle dormitory. The other girls had shied away from her when she'd returned, assuming that she was as shocked and scared as Bernadette had been. Probably as dozens — hundreds — of girls had been. But Emmaline was neither shocked nor scared. No more than anyone who had spent the day feeding snarling prehistoric beasts would be, at any rate. Josie had shown that she didn't give a fig about their fierce jaws and flapping wings. At least within the cage they were manageable. She recalled the look on Rab's face last night as he'd gripped her window ledge. When flying or hunting, the pterodactyls were another matter entirely.

Josie gave Emmaline hope. The ungainly, fearless girl amazed her. The school depended on keeping the girls laden down with fear. Josie didn't have any. She was simple in the best way: uncomplicated, not bothered by things like, "Why are there flying dinosaurs here?" but instead thinking, "Why should I be afraid of those strange birds when I can hit them with a bucket or a hockey stick?" She didn't care about Matron or Mrs. Wackett, either. What could they do to her? Really? Whatever they did, it didn't bother her.

Emmaline had heard that Josie's parents had been eaten

by lions. That was why she'd been at St. Grimelda's since she was ten years old. She'd be here until she was eighteen. There were no relatives she could go to. There was only some kind of trustee with the Church Missionary Society in London, a kind of legal guardian, who paid her fees for the school. She had also heard something about Josie coming into an inheritance when she reached eighteen.

But this was just gossip, of course, and Josie had not talked about it at all. Still, it made sense. Josie didn't have anywhere else to go. But she didn't have to put up with any nonsense, wherever she was.

And she was willing to help Emmaline, who did have somewhere else to go.

That night, for the first time since she had arrived at St. Grimelda's, Emmaline slept soundly.

"No Gypsies allowed here!" shouted the landlord of the Sunny View Hotel. Madame ZaZa had knocked on the front door, bold as brass, crying, "Tell your fortunes!"

It was a ruse, of course. Madame ZaZa didn't want to tell the landlord's fortune but to let Rubberbones know that she wanted to speak with him.

She left with a good deal of loud shouting in Romany (curses, no doubt) and stamped down the high street in obvious bad humor. Rubberbones, running down the lane behind the hotel, met her at the corner. Her quarrelsomeness disappeared into peals of laughter.

"Oh, that was fun! I'm glad I didn't have to read that 'orrid man's fortune — I'm sure that it's exactly what you'd expect! Miserable old coot! Fetch that nice lady and the Indian gentleman, my duck, and meet us under the oak tree by the cemetery. About half an hour? We've brought friends — and a few ideas of our own."

"Aye!" said Rab. "I'll bring 'em along."

"Oh, and dearie, how would you feel about dressing up as one of us — a Romany — to play a trick up at the school?"

Rab thought about it for something less than a quarter of a second. What was there not to like about it?

"That'd be champion!" he replied.

"And we might need fireworks. We have a friend who makes excellent ones. You don't mind fireworks, do you?"

The boy grinned from ear to ear. All he could want now was another piece of Madame ZaZa's chocolate cake.

The girl had seen a newspaper. The school forbade all word from outside, but there had been some pieces of crumpled paper as wrapping in a box of new plates for the dining room. She'd been told to unpack the china by Matron. Miss Scantcommon (the girl could barely pronounce the strange name) did not notice as she took the newspaper and hid it under her skirt. She read it later, in secret, making out the words slowly. There was a page of something called "Foreign News," and in it she found a piece about a place called Chiligrit. There was trouble in Chiligrit. She knew the names mentioned. They were her relatives. Some of them were her enemies. One of them wanted to take the throne, which was hers by right.

She decided it was time to leave this horrible school. But this was easier said than done.

<hr>

The caravan was drawn up by the ancient tree, as Madame ZaZa had said it would be. Aunt Lucy, Lal Singh and Rab had come on foot. Although it was two in the afternoon there was an air of secrecy about the meeting. Sid ushered them inside the wagon. It was a tight fit; Romany caravans aren't made for gatherings of seven people.

Norah made the introductions.

"I'd like you to meet my nephew, Rollo." She gestured at a dark, elfin-faced boy of perhaps fifteen, in shirt and neckerchief. "He's offered to assist us. And this is my friend Professor Bellbuckle, who has amazin' skills as wot might suit our needs."

There wasn't room in the caravan for anyone to bow or kiss hands, but the thin, pale man with the long gray hair brushed back from his high forehead would have done so if he could.

"Charmed, dear ladies, gentlemen."

"The professor is a scientific experimentalist," said Madame ZaZa.

"Merely a student of natural philosophy and developmental engineering," explained Professor Bellbuckle. "With an interest in the pioneering aspects of propulsive invention. That and the incendiary and illuminative qualities of certain explosive mixtures. In short, I am a mad scientist."

He smiled, showing crumbs in his gray beard. Chocolate cake, Rubberbones noticed, with interest.

"I resisted the use of that title for many years, preferring more dignified, scientific terms, but my whole family referred to me in even more unfortunate descriptions for many years, and I have come to embrace the term 'mad scientist' as an honor. Indeed, those were the words that the *Savannah Morning News* chose to employ in my regard after the 'Gaston Square Incident.' My family used to own a house there, you see. Gaston Square. Before the incident."

Rubberbones was fascinated by the way this man spoke. His turn of phrase and his accent. It was soft and drawn out in odd places. Perhaps he was Welsh.

"You'd be an American, then?" asked Aunt Lucy, who knew Welsh when she heard it.

"Yes, ma'am," replied the courteous professor. "Born and raised in Savannah, Georgia, educated at several fine institutions in Georgia and the Carolinas, currently living here, after several years of traveling extensively at the request of my family and loved ones."

Rubberbones couldn't quite work out what that meant. Professor Bellbuckle saw this from his expression.

"It means that they provide me with large amounts of money so long as I promise not to return. Until they invite me, which they haven't. They dislike my works. Especially my fireworks."

Sid cleared his throat. "We 'ave to decide what to do to get young Emmaline out of that . . . that *school*." He used the word as if it were a curse. "Aunt Lucy's arranged for a servant at the school to take a message to her, and bring one back, but 'less we have a plan of some kind, there's not a lot we can tell 'er."

"We can ask her if there is anything she needs," suggested Aunt Lucy. "She might have ideas of her own."

"Good point, dearie," said Madame ZaZa. "She's not a helpless baby. She might indeed have plans. She might just need something to help."

"Could we send her a parcel? You know, like putting a file inside a cake, like as prisoners get, sometimes?" This was young Rollo, bright-eyed.

"Alas, the school has a strict policy about post, parcels and the like," said Aunt Lucy. "The girls aren't allowed anything at all."

"What if . . . what if we found out what she needed and smuggled it in some other way?" asked Rollo. He was a crafty one, thought Rubberbones admiringly.

"We can send the message to find out," said Aunt Lucy. "It never hurts to ask."

Madame ZaZa brought out a chocolate cake — Rubberbones thought that producing cakes so easily was some sort of Gypsy magic — and Aunt Lucy told everyone the whole story as she knew it. The American professor listened politely, making notes in a leather-bound book. He noticed the boy peering over his shoulder. Rab was looking at sketches of very strange objects.

"That's the Bellbuckle Patent Mole Drill, Mark II, son. It looks like a small steam engine with a giant screw on the front. I built it last year in South Africa. The engineer gets up a head o' steam like a locomotive, which powers the wheels, and also" — he pointed at the screw — "the digging device, here. I designed it to burrow through layers of rock. If I had it here, we could dig a tunnel under the walls of that old school in no time at all."

"That'd be champion!" Rubberbones was excited.

"It would indeed," replied Professor Bellbuckle, "but, sadly, the machine has been impounded in South Africa, owing to a minor — and entirely unpredictable — accident. The shaft of a diamond mine collapsed when I drove into it. No one informed me it was there. Nobody was hurt, fortunately, but the owners felt that I was somehow responsible for the damage. In short, they kept the Mole Drill because I wouldn't pay 'em for wrecking their gosh-darn mine shaft, which was built on pretty flimsy principles, if you ask me."

Lal Singh looked at Rab with an expression that suggested the professor was, in fact, a complete lunatic.

"All right, listen, dearies," said Norah. "I've got a cunning plan in mind. Rab 'as offered to dress up in costume for it. Just listen to my scheme."

So they listened. It was a cunning plan indeed.

CHAPTER 19

In Which Emmaline Becomes Violent

Emmaline was being "a good girl." At least, that was what her mother would have called her. She was attentive in class, devoted to her chores and active in Miss Sharpelbow's games. Mrs. Wackett might have thought that her most difficult pupil had become a model "gel."

It was all a ruse. Emmaline was planning another escape. This time it would work, and she had someone to help her. Someone trustworthy. Josie.

Emmaline had thought that the first thing to do was to bring Rab's broken kite inside.

"That way we can examine it and see if we can use it again," Emmaline said to Josie. "It might not be completely smashed. There must be something worth salvaging!"

Emmaline was quite eager to retrieve the kite. Josie thought there was something else to be done first.

"'S all very well to say that, Emmaline. Climb out on the roof and fetch the dratted thing in. Not a problem at all. So we gets the kite in through the window all nice and quiet, and nobody spots us, right?"

"Right," said Emmaline, thinking that it might be a bit more of a problem than that.

"Well, what then? We take it into your dorm and have Amelia fetch Scantcommon, just to spite you? Or Hannah 'confess' to the first teacher who catches her doing something wrong? Or take it up to the fifth-form dorm, where the fifth-form girls who act just like Amelia and Hannah will do the exact same thing?"

"No," said Emmaline. "Of course not!"

"Got to use our loaves, see!" Josie tapped the side of her head. "My dad used to say that if you don't use your loaf you'll be in trouble. We can't just drag the kite into plain sight of everyone. We have to hide it, first off, then have somewhere to work on fixing it up."

Emmaline knew that Josie was right. No wonder Josie didn't care about the rules and the punishments and the general daily oppressions. She just thought her way around them. "Where, then?"

Josie grinned. "Got just the place in mind. Somewhere with big cupboards to put things in, where a lot of people go, but nobody stays very long. Except me."

"Josie, now you're just teasing me! What are you talking about?"

"Upstairs. The equipment room for the Ball Game. You know, where I was when I mistook your pal Rab for a witch on a broomstick! Miss Sharpelbow made me games captain last year. I spend time cleaning the kit and fixing things that are broke and keeping track of the supplies and stuff like that. It gives me a reason to stay away from the snobby girls. I have a place and time to think and be on me own, and that's nice."

Emmaline realized that Josie's stubborn independence went hand in hand with the loneliness of being one who never fitted in. Until she herself had met Aunt Lucy and Lal Singh and the strange, wonderful boy who bounced, she had always felt the same.

"Now," continued Josie, "everyone knows that I love the Ball Game. Nobody questions how come I spend half my free time in the kit room. You don't spend your time cleaning hockey sticks or counting knee pads — never knew we had knee pads, did you? You need to develop a tremendous enthusiasm for the game."

Emmaline grimaced. "It's extremely violent."

"Yeah, great, isn't it?" replied Josie.

"But I hate it," said Emmaline.

"All right, *pretend* you love it, then. Decide that it's the best thing ever invented. Want to form a league within the school, have tournaments, that sort of thing. Then I'll ask Sharpelbow if you can help me with the equipment."

"Won't it seem odd to her that I have suddenly developed this love of hitting people with a stick and bouncing a ball off walls?"

"Not at all. She won't think about it that way," said Josie. "See, Sharpelbow thinks the Ball Game is terrific. Builds character, she says. But most of the girls hate it as much as you do. Only me and that little girl I almost ran into seem to like it much."

"What little girl? Charlotte?"

"No, not her. Gwendolyn. The one as cracks her knuckles so much."

Emmaline gasped. "She's not little at all. She's twice my size!"

"Well, I'm three times your size. Everyone's little to me. Anyway, point is, Sharpelbow will be pleased as punch. I'll tell her that you got interested the day you sent me flying head over heels. Sharpelbow will go for that. 'Sonly reasonable you'd enjoy a game where you could injure people bigger'n you!"

Emmaline seriously doubted that this would make sense to anyone except Josie or Miss Sharpelbow. But the next day she and Josie went out early on the Ball Game court to practice. It hurt. A lot. They did this every day for a week.

"Ouch!" said Emmaline as Josie lashed her across the knees with her stick.

"Good fun, isn't it?" Josie grinned.

"Aaaagh!" cried Emmaline as her friend hooked her ankle and twisted it.

"Better watch out. You can't grow another leg!" shouted Josie. Emmaline slipped and swung her own stick wildly. Josie grunted and toppled over.

"Oh, crumbs! Did I hit you on the head?" asked Emmaline.

"Yeah, really hurt, that one did. Keep up the good work!" said Josie, getting up. Her head was bleeding a little.

Miss Sharpelbow was impressed.

At the end of the week, she appointed Emmaline deputy games captain. It was a great honor, apparently. Emmaline smiled and did a little curtsy.

"Don't push your luck," whispered Josie.

———

Rubberbones should have been frustrated. It was more than a week since the disastrous episode with the giant birds. The cunning plan seemed to develop slowly. Lal Singh had taken the dogcart back to Lower Owlthwaite to check on the old house on the hill, tend to the garden and generally look after things. He'd also taken a note for Mrs. Burns, Rab's gran, to let her know where he was. Aunt Lucy and Rubberbones remained at the Sunny View Hotel as its only guests. Sid and Norah had disappeared into the countryside.

But, actually, Rab was enjoying spending most of his time with the mad American inventor. Professor Bellbuckle had a cottage right on the edge of the cliffs just outside Fishwick. It wasn't much of a cottage, but it had several sheds of different sizes attached to it, and mad scientists need sheds.

The professor's sheds were full of experiments, pieces for future experiments and bits of past experiments that had

gone wrong. He also had boxes of homemade fireworks; he liked fireworks and thought the ones sold in shops were much too feeble.

"This is my patent submersible single-mariner craft," explained Bellbuckle. "What some might call a submarine. I have hopes for it." Rab's eyes grew large at the sight of a metal cylinder, flattened slightly on top, with a periscope and two pairs of matching paddles on either side. It had brass handles. The top opened like a casket.

"The submariner lies inside the body of the vessel, looking through the periscope, which is set at an angle so he can see while lying on his back. One set of paddles is operated by the feet, using a bicycle mechanism, while the other pair is wound by the hands. You steer it like those little boats at the park, peddling just one side so it turns about. What do you think?"

Rubberbones couldn't decide what it was that made him nervous. Few things made Robert Burns nervous. Certainly the idea of an experimental submarine that operated by hand-cranked paddles was appealing.

Then it struck him. "It looks like a coffin!" he exclaimed.

The professor sighed. "Yes, darn it, it surely does. That's what the group of investors said. I had hoped they'd put their faith and fortunes into this project. But, you know, people don't want to be associated with anything that looks like a coffin. Unless, I suppose, they are in the undertakerin' line of business."

"Does it work, though?" asked Rab.

"Well, son, I don't rightly know. I'm too tall to fit in this here model, and I can't bring myself to ask anyone to pilot a submarine that looks like a coffin. Too many experimental vessels have turned out to be exactly that. There was a submersible that I was associated with in my youth — during an unfortunate episode in the history of my country known as the War between the States, which some ignorant persons persist in calling the Civil War — that became a casket for the crew. A very sad affair."

Rab looked up at the tall American. "I'd give it a go, if you like!"

Professor Bellbuckle patted him on the shoulder. "I appreciate your offer, son. Maybe another time. It's pretty cold in the North Sea this time of year. Besides, I have a passel of other things to show you."

The professor pulled out a big box marked "DANGER! EXPLOSIVES!" Rab stared in shocked disbelief as Bellbuckle shook it violently. "Good," he said. "I was worried it would blow up in our faces."

It was a dark — though not stormy — night, ideal for secrecy. It was a night for sneaking out of bed, climbing out of a window, onto a ledge and down to a roof. The two adventuresses moved carefully, to avoid prying classmates, wandering teachers and tripping over the dormitory furniture.

"I've done this before," whispered Josie as she helped Emmaline out of the equipment room window.

"Lots of times?" asked Emmaline.

"Well, no, once — when I broke my nose rescuing a stray kitten from the roof."

This wasn't comforting news, and Emmaline didn't ask for the whole story. It could wait. She was desperately trying to follow Josie along the narrow ledge, where one course of stones met another on the tower wall. They kept their backs to the wall, hands carefully gripping the shapes of the stone blocks. The wind bit at Emmaline's face. She wished for warmer clothes than the gym kit she had put on; still, it was better to be cold in practical clothes than in the heavy, tight garments that she wore for classes. She looked about, peering into the blackness. For what? The pterodactyls? Perhaps. If they were flying tonight, they had an advantage over her. The night sky was their domain; they would be far more frightening than in the close confines of their cage. Emmaline listened for the beating of wings, the shrill cry of the flying beasts. She heard nothing. Josie was confident, pushing ahead. She carried herself as she did in the Ball Game; nothing dared stop her advance. Emmaline wondered whether a thirty-foot drop would bother Josie at all. They reached the angle of the main school block. A chink of light from a window showed the way. Josie helped Emmaline down onto the slate roof.

"There it is. The kite. Blimey, it is a bit bashed up. Oh well. Help me hoist it onto my back, and we'll see what it looks like in the light. Let's go back the way we came," said Josie.

Josie, with the twisted canvas frame flapping behind her, seemed to have no difficulty retracing her steps. She folded the kite through the window and slipped through into the equipment room. Emmaline followed gingerly, heart in mouth.

The kite wasn't broken completely, but it wasn't in great condition, either. It had been rent in three places by giant flying carnivores and had been stuck on a roof for several days of wind and English autumn rain. The whole new wing that Rab had lashed to it had gone. It looked a bit crumpled and pathetic.

"It's like an old umbrella you might see in the street after a cart has run over it," said Josie.

Emmaline nodded. "Yes, but sometimes you just need an umbrella. Any umbrella."

CHAPTER 20

Training Stanley

Emmaline was surprised when one of the school servants — a shy, surly woman from a village nearby — slipped a note to her while she was on kitchen duties. "Get me an answer before the day's out and I'll get it to yer family," whispered the woman.

Emmaline slipped the tightly folded piece of paper into a pocket until she had a chance to read it in private. She had a moment while she was in the pantry.

Dear Emmaline — We are trying to devise a plan to get you out. Those nice Gypsies that took in young Robert are helping us, and they have a very pleasant scientific gentleman from America along to assist. We are staying in Fishwick so as to be close to you. We have money, fireworks, rope, cardboard, glue and true predictions of the future. Apparently, we have a submarine as well, though the professor says it may simply be a box that sinks. However, we have no actual scheme in mind as of yet, so if there's anything you have thought of (or need) let me know and we'll do what we can. The person who bears this note will bring your reply to us as we have bribed her with money (jolly exciting, isn't it?). Love always, Aunt Lucy.

P.S. Lal Singh sends his best regards, as do Robert and the horse.

It was quite an odd sort of letter, but then, Aunt Lucy was an odd of sort of relative. Emmaline wrote her reply on the back of the note, stealing extra minutes when she was supposed to be counting bottles of Everglue's Spicy Condimental Sauce ("Since 1834, None More Spicy," as the label said).

Dear Aunt Lucy — Am planning to rebuild Rab's kite and hope for the best. I've a friend here to help me. I can get glue and string. What I want is heavy brown paper and some thin wooden rods. What I need most is a net to land the thing in, as (unlike Rab) I expect that I should break various bits of me without one. Also, need a way to let you know when I'm to do it — must run — love, Emmaline.

The servant took the folded note without a word or change of expression. Emmaline returned to the pantry and found that there were seventy-nine bottles of Everglue's Spicy Condimental Sauce in store, enough to disguise the taste of St. Grimelda's horrible food for about three weeks.

Rab enjoyed dressing up like a Gypsy. He wore a brocade waistcoat, a red kerchief round his head and a yellow one round his neck. He looked like a Romany boy in a play rather than a real one, which was Madame ZaZa's plan all along. Rollo looked him up and down.

"You'll do, *gorgio* boy, as long as you keep your mouth shut. Another Romany would know you for a fake, but for today's work, you'll be fine."

Lal Singh had returned from Lower Owlthwaite with a friend who was going to be vital to the plan. This friend jumped down and started licking Rubberbones on the face.

"Oh! Watch out, yer daft dog!"

It was Stanley, the vicar's enthusiastic mongrel. Lal Singh had borrowed him while the vicar, now retired, was taking a holiday with his elderly sister. She lived in the Suffolk town of Frinton, which was three train rides away from Lower Owlthwaite. Stanley was inclined to misbehave on trains. He was also inclined to misbehave toward the vicar's sister, who couldn't understand why her brother kept a small, grinning dog of mixed ancestry and worse behavior. So, Stanley was given into Lal Singh's care for a few weeks. Lal Singh, as always, had a plan of his own.

"Look, Rab-sahib, I have trained the dog."

He took a ball from his pocket and threw it high over the caravan. Stanley leaped after it, going under the wagon. He pursued the ball with a bouncing sort of run. He picked it up. He came back with it. He dropped it at Lal Singh's feet.

"All dogs do that, don't they, Mr. Lal Singh?" said Rab.

"All dogs do, indeed," replied the Sikh. "But I have taught him to be doing this in a way most valuable to our requirements. Rab-sahib, would you go to that cottage over there, knock on the door and ask whoever opens the door for the precise time of the clock. Or a drink of water. Something unsuspicious and everyday."

Rab went over to a brick cottage by the side of the road. He tapped on the door. The door opened after a few moments, and a sharp-faced woman appeared.

"Er, hello —" began Rab.

The old lady said abruptly, "Not today, boy. No Gypsies allowed here!"

Lal Singh, standing at the garden gate, immediately threw the ball right over the top of the house.

Stanley leaped after it. He didn't try to climb the cottage wall, of course — no dog would do that. He didn't run around the cottage, as most dogs would. He ran straight at the open door, pushing past the woman in his rush to get to the ball. He raced through the perfectly kept cottage, tried to paw his way through the closed back door, knocked over the milk jug and upset a basket of potatoes.

The housewife was furious. Lal Singh apologized and gave the woman a golden guinea for her trouble.

Lal Singh smiled at Rubberbones. "You see, I have trained the dog. Tomorrow we will use his training."

The kite was tucked away in one of the big cabinets in the equipment room. Emmaline and Josie had decided that it was best to concentrate on their lessons until they knew whether Aunt Lucy was going to send the things they needed.

Emmaline found her class work generally easy. She noticed that Miss Silverspoon had not yet recovered from seeing Rubberbones floating outside her window; the teacher seemed to be on the verge of panic, although it was unclear what there was to panic about while teaching embroidery. Latin class was harder — all irregular verbs and something called conjugations. Emmaline didn't know what those things were. Nobody else did, either, but it didn't seem to matter. Latin was what they call a "dead language"; it seemed unlikely that an actual Roman would drop by to chat. The teacher, Miss Venividivici, seemed ancient enough to have known Julius Caesar in person. She'd probably have rapped his knuckles with a ruler, too, because her temper was something fierce.

Hannah had tried to make up for telling on Emmaline.

"I am really, truly sorry I told Wackett about your scheme. But I had to. She made all kinds of horrible threats, and I knew I'd just die if I didn't get to go home for Christmas."

Emmaline smiled. "It's all right, Hannah. I shouldn't have dragged you in."

But it wasn't all right, of course.

There was no point in blaming Hannah. There was also no point in trusting Hannah. When someone's loyalty to a friend snaps as easily as Hannah's had in Mrs. Wackett's office, it's best to simply remember that. So Emmaline said, "Don't worry, Hannah. No more ridiculous schemes for me. I've certainly learned my lesson!"

It was true. But it was not the lesson Hannah might have imagined.

The Gypsy wagon rolled along the track toward the school, its green and red paintwork glistening in the October sunlight. Moving slowly and easily was Sid's intention, so as to avoid suspicion. Moving slowly, though not all that easily, was the horse's decision, for the caravan was heavier than usual today.

Sid drove. Inside were Madame ZaZa, Rubberbones and Stanley. Rollo walked beside the horse. Professor Bellbuckle had wanted to come along with his Patent Explosive Petard, Model 1887. The professor had explained this as "an ingenious device, which, clamped to a door, wall or similar and operated by a simple fuse or timer, exerts the full force of its explosive charge, of dynamite or similar, onto the designated object without expending unnecessary energy in other directions."

What this meant was not completely clear to Rubberbones. He did understand that a big explosion was part of whatever the professor had in mind. That was all right as far as he was concerned.

"Champion!" Rubberbones had cried out in enthusiasm. "Marvello!" agreed Rollo.

"Absolutely not!" "No! No! No!" "You'll get us all arrested!" shouted Aunt Lucy, Madame ZaZa and Sid, all at the same time.

Professor Bellbuckle looked crestfallen. "I guess y'all are right. It did get me arrested. Helena, Montana, spring of '88. And at the Vatican library in 1890. Seems there's a lot of folks don't appreciate a real good explosion. Most of them that do are bank robbers, and that don't ever turn out well. I prefer the company of honest folks, mostly."

So he had stayed at his cottage, making fireworks and strange devices of clockwork and steam, and said he'd see them all for supper. Aunt Lucy stayed with him, to keep him company and prevent anything dangerous from happening. She'd taken a liking to the professor, and decided that he needed looking after. The rest of the party went on, according to their scheme.

Everything went exactly as planned. Well, almost.

CHAPTER 21

No Gypsies Allowed!

"Baskets for sale! Knives made sharp as new!" Rollo sang out in a fine, clear voice.

Mr. Pinchbeak's face appeared at the tiny window cut into the double gates of St. Grimelda's. "Clear off! No thieving Gypsies here!"

Madame ZaZa stuck her head out of the wagon. "Read yer fortune, dearie?"

"No!" roared Pinchbeak. "I told you to be on your way! I'll set the bir — I'll have the law on you for trespassin'!"

Hidden in the caravan, Rab grinned to himself. He knew that Pinchbeak was going to say "set the birds on you!" but then likely remembered he wasn't supposed to mention them. They were the school's secret weapon, no doubt about it. He scratched Stanley between the ears. "Almost ready, boy."

Rab could hear Madame ZaZa bantering with Pinchbeak. "I can foretell your future, dearie. One part of it. You are going to get in trouble 'cos of the girl what's run off."

"Give over," replied Pinchbeak. "Ain't no girls run off from 'ere. Not today, not ever."

"We saw somebody — a slip of a girl — running across the moor. Lost a shoe she did, and snagged her clothes."

"No, never!" shouted Pinchbeak, agitated. "Never passed the gate."

"I'm not saying she did," said Madame ZaZa. "I'm just saying you'll get the blame however she got loose. The shoe is just over there —" She jabbed her finger at a tuft of gorse bush some distance off. "I think it's part of a cloak on that bit o' bush."

Which was right, because Rollo had put those things — bought for pennies at a charity shop in Fishwick — exactly where Madame ZaZa had said, about ten minutes before.

Pinchbeak did exactly what the old Romany woman knew he would. He opened the small door in great excitement and ran toward the wagon.

"Over there, mate!" cried Sid, from up on the driver's seat. The gatekeeper couldn't see where he meant. "Just a few minutes gone by." Pinchbeak scurried around the caravan.

As he passed Rollo, the boy stepped on the gatekeeper's foot and shoved him onto the grass. "Whoops! Ever so sorry, sir! Let me help you get up!" Rollo could be very polite when it suited him. He was signaling to Rab, who had been peering through the window in the caravan.

In an instant, Rab was out of the vehicle. Stanley was at his feet, leaping with joy. The ball flashed as Rab threw it high over the school wall. "Go, boy!" he whispered.

Go was what Stanley did. The little dog raced for the open gate, a furry streak of lightning. Rab was behind him, shouting, "Come back! Come back right now!"

Pinchbeak turned round to see the dog dash through the gateway, a Gypsy boy five steps behind him. "Stop right there!" he bellowed. Rollo caught him in the back of the knee with a foot, sending him back into the muddy grass. "Whoops, did I knock you over again? Ever so sorry, sir. I'll catch that rascal dog!"

And, so saying, was fast running into the school himself.

———

Emmaline was in mathematics class when the uproar began. The girls sitting by the window noticed it first. A commotion in the quad. Old Miss Sumfiddle was never really able to exert much authority over her pupils, so it was a matter of moments before all the girls were at the window. Emmaline was not the first girl there, but by using Josie's Ball Game techniques, she was able to push her way to a good view of what was going on. What she saw was this:

A small dog, running madly, was disappearing among the outbuildings on the far side of the quad.

A small boy, dressed like a pantomime pirate, was chasing the dog. He quickly seemed to lose track of the animal and ran in and out of the sheds shouting and waving his arms about.

Another boy, taller and older ("Ooh, he's a handsome one!" called out one of the girls behind her), followed, running around the quad, searching in the alcoves of the main school block and then looking up at the windows.

Emmaline realized he wasn't looking for the dog. He was looking up at the window upon window of schoolgirls who were admiring him. He was, Emmaline admitted, a good-

looking boy, with dark hair and eyes and a slim body in Romany clothes.

Romany clothes. She looked across to see the smaller boy; his clothing seemed somehow artificial, with blond hair sticking out from under a headcloth. He made some kind of hand signal to the black-haired youth. She knew him.

Rubberbones!

The older boy put one hand to his lips and whistled. The small dog appeared once again, apparently from nowhere. Pinchbeak hobbled through the gateway, dirty and angry. Miss Scantcommon marched across the quad, looking determined.

The older boy waved a hand in a gesture of apology to Miss Scantcommon while Rubberbones and the dog ran past Pinchbeak and out of the school gate. Pinchbeak tried to smack Rab's head as he went by, but the dog leaped at him and the gatekeeper recoiled in fear. The slender youth waved at his audience, bowed slightly and followed them out through the gateway. Pinchbeak scowled. Miss Scantcommon stood with legs apart, hands on hips. You could tell she was angry, even without seeing her face. A girl in another window cheered and others whistled. Matron turned around, eyes furious, and the noise ceased immediately.

Emmaline stepped back from the window as Miss Sumfiddle grumbled about decorum and proper manners and "these young gels today!"

"All very odd. Very interesting," thought Emmaline. "And wasn't that the vicar's little dog?"

———

"Excellent work all round!" declared Sid. "Though frankly, Rollo, it ain't necessary to bow to all those young ladies as if you'd just finished playing Hamlet in front of the royal family. Those teachers are a suspicious lot, so don't give 'em reason to look twice at you. Remember, next trip to the school can't be a circus like this one. We have to look quite *unobtrusive* if we want it to work."

They were all sitting around the table at the professor's cottage. He had cleared it of springs, tubes, coils and clockworky bits for the occasion.

Sid continued, "Rab, what did you find when you explored those sheds?"

"Lots o' places with boxes and barrels, some empty cabins, some bits o' wood and a place where they pile up rubbish for burning," replied Rubberbones. "There's one wi' a green door, with shelves of boxes and tools. I think an extra box or two might not get spotted by anyone who didn't know as to look for 'em."

"That sounds like a splendid hiding place," said Aunt Lucy. "What are we going to send Emmaline, then? Let's make a list."

They jotted down the things she had mentioned: brown paper, lengths of thin round wood known as "doweling," along with some scissors and a sharp knife. Lal Singh, the old soldier, suggested a good map of the whole area. Aunt Lucy thought a cake made of tasty roots and dried fruit would be a nice addition. The professor said he'd come up with some useful inventions to tuck in if they allowed him a day or two. Rubberbones said, "Fireworks."

"Fireworks?" said Aunt Lucy.

"Fireworks?" said Sid.

"Aye, fireworks," Rab replied. "To send up and let us know she's coming. To shoot off at them leathery birds. To warn us if she needs to. And just because!"

This seemed to make a lot of sense and, besides, everyone likes fireworks. They went down on the list, which grew longer and longer. Madame ZaZa pointed out that a huge package containing a balloon and basket, maps of the world, cake for a month and a big box of fireworks might be a bit obvious. They crossed off a few things, like a wooly hat to keep Emmaline's ears warm and a pair of sun goggles (which had been Rab's addition, because he liked them and had never had a chance to try any on).

How to smuggle this parcel to Emmaline, though? Aunt Lucy had the answer for that. "The grocer's van. It goes up there once a week, rain or shine."

"We could steal it!" said Rollo. "And do a big breakout of Emmaline and all those girls who were looking at me!"

"We could drug the grocer with a patent medicine I'd mix up," said Professor Bellbuckle.

"We could get the grocer and his lad drunk on cider in the pub and borrow the van when they are sleeping it off," said Sid.

"We could paint the caravan to look like the grocer's van, and they wouldn't know it was us!" cried Rubberbones. He was getting a bit carried away.

Lal Singh said nothing, but it was clear none of these ideas appealed to him.

Madame ZaZa shook her head. "Too complicated by half."

Aunt Lucy smiled. "The grocer is old and short-sighted. He has a boy with him, a mischievous lad with red hair. I expect he might be up for a practical joke. He'd probably do it for a bottle of ginger beer and a good laugh afterwards. Rollo, Robert, you two need to meet him. I'll show you where the shop is. He finishes at six o'clock."

Sometimes it's good to have a mad old lady who noses about asking a lot of questions.

———

Everyone except Emmaline was fast asleep. She knew that her friends were up to something. She also knew that the school staff were not fools, and that they did not believe in coincidences. Matron and Mrs. Wackett and that horrible gate-keeping dwarf would be on the lookout. It was time for great care. She crept to the window. The stars were bright, the sky a deep blue. And, if it was not her imagination playing tricks, there was something else out there. Wheeling across the night sky, calling to one another, were those prehistoric creatures that everyone simply called "the birds."

CHAPTER 22

Ginger Beer and Everglue's Spicy Condimental Sauce

Albert Baggett was fifteen, freckled and a bit rodenty about the teeth. He had worked for the village grocer, "Thos. Appleburr, Groceries and Provisions, Established 1867," for two years and found it lacking in entertainment value. That was more or less what he told Rab and Rollo. Actually, what he said was, "Old Appleburr's blind as a bat, deaf as a post and spends all his time quoting the Old Testament at me 'bout things I might do against the will of the Almighty. Mostly that's about me trying to 'ave a bit of fun sometimes. Old Appleburr is dead set against people 'aving fun. Says it's against scripture to 'ave a bit of fun."

Rollo had bought bottles of ginger beer for all three of them, and they sat on a stile at the edge of Fishwick. Rollo had devised a cunning plan. Rab was amazed, as he had never devised a cunning plan in his life.

"See, Albert, it's like this. You know the girls' school up on the moor?" said Rollo.

"Aye. We deliver there every Wednesday, Old Appleburr and me. Course, I do all the lifting and carrying, while 'e goes over the account with that 'orrible matron woman."

"Well, see, Albert, I have a . . . a sister what stays there, and I want to get a message to her," said Rollo.

This was a lie, of course. It was a very obvious lie, because

Albert wouldn't believe that this Romany boy who traveled about in a painted caravan would have a sister at the school. Not even as a servant there.

"Oh, yes!" said Albert, raising an eyebrow. "A sister! Of course, mate. I understand completely!"

What he understood was that Rollo wanted to get a message to a girl he was sweet on. Albert knew all about that; there were half a dozen girls that he tried to talk with while Old Appleburr wasn't paying attention. He was already on Rollo's side. It was a much better story than the one that went, "I am trying to smuggle parts for a flying machine into the school, so a girl I don't know can build it and escape." Which goes to show how the world really works.

"I'll take your letter, don't worry!" said Albert.

"No," said Rollo. "I have a better plan. I've got her a present — a parcel, like — and we have a secret place to keep things up at the school. I can't go myself, because the folk there would recognize me —"

"I'll bet they would," said Albert with a big grin and a wink.

"So I want Rab here," Rollo went on, pointing at Rubberbones, "to sneak it to that secret place. Maybe while you are unloading the van and the grocer is doing his orders list with that matron. Could you help us?"

"Oh, aye, lad. 'Appen I've got a cap and an apron that don't fit me no more. Yon lad could ride in t'back with the deliveries and hop out once we get to the school. Wednesday morning — that's tomorrow, then."

So they worked out exactly how to do it.

———⊸•⊷———

Professor Bellbuckle was pottering about in his laboratory. Miss Lucy, as he had come to call her, had made it clear that none of his larger inventions could be smuggled by a small boy into the school, let alone be hidden in a store shed. He had that same small boy with him right now. And a small dog, because Stanley had become Rubberbones's boon companion by this time.

"This model is the Bellbuckle Steam Propulsive Engine, Model 1891," explained the inventor. "It uses a turbine system of my own devising and is a considerable improvement on qwall models in use anywhere today. Has the power of four hundred horses."

Rubberbones looked at it with astonishment. It was the size of a clock. "Amazing, Professor! Can you use it in a boat or a flying machine?"

Rab could see the professor make a sort of harrumphing motion in his throat.

"This is just the model. It actually has the power of, well, several mice. The real thing is the size of my cottage; a little bit larger, in fact. It was confiscated from me by the police in Vienna three years ago, after an . . . an *incident* with the emperor's river launch. The Austrian ruler is an old man with no imagination at all. A forward-thinking monarch would want to zip up and down the Danube River like a hungry alligator after a raftfull of orphans, but not this nincompoop! Anyway, I didn't mean to sink his boat. Sacrifices in the name of science!"

They were both quiet for a moment, the professor missing his steam engine and Rab wondering if there was any cake to be had.

"Here is an actual clockwork engine I made," continued Professor Bellbuckle. "This would propel a flyer perfectly well, but only if the pilot was very light indeed. I haven't met this Emmaline of yours, but I assume she's bigger than, say, a good-sized chicken?"

Rab thought about it for a moment. "Aye," he replied. "Bigger than any chicken I've ever seen."

The professor opened an old wooden chest. He pulled

out a folder of papers and old photographs, mildewed and eaten by insects.

"Here we are! Devices for swimming. Devices for floating. This is more the kind of thing we could help Emmaline with. See this one? An invention from 1870; I ferget the name of the fella as made it. It's a rubber suit with a cork band around the middle to aid flotation and lead weights round the ankles to keep you upright. You have to ensure, of course, that the cork helps you float more than the lead makes you sink. See the separate waterproof container for sandwiches, cigars and a newspaper? What? No, I don't imagine Emmaline smokes cigars. Here's another device, basically a bicycle with a propeller that you lean forward into and — well, yes, I do admit there is some minor risk of drowning. But that's what I am leading up to: the Bellbuckle Patent Life Saver Apparatus, Mark III!"

He pulled a black oilskin bag from the chest. "Size small! Cork inserts, rubber bodysuit, propellers on the feet that flip back when not in use, belt for lashing yourself to suitable wreckage. No cigars, though. There's room for fireworks and matches and just maybe sandwiches in this pocket, too!"

Rab thought for a moment. "I think a nice slab o' cake 'd be better."

———

Emmaline volunteered to stay on kitchen duties rather than switch with another girl to do the next task on the list, which was dusting the portraits of headmistresses of long ago, fierce harridans immortalized by terrified artists. This was unusual, since most girls hated kitchen chores as much as anything.

"Really?" said the girl, a Remove with thick, round spectacles.

"Really," said Emmaline. "I like to count the bottles of sauce. It's very — erm — relaxing. And it teaches arithmetic."

The surly woman who worked in the kitchen brought a note on Tuesday morning. Once again, Emmaline retreated to the cupboard full of Everglue's Spicy Condimental Sauce ("None More Saucy") to read the message.

Dear Emmaline — We are sending you a parcel this coming Wednesday, by way of the grocer's van. Rab will put the package inside the store shed with the green door, if that means anything to you; if it doesn't you must go and find out where it is. We are sending everything you asked for and whatever else we could think of, though not the really big things like a mattress to land on or a rocket. We are sending fireworks. Professor Bellbuckle will say a bit about them.

Here the handwriting changed.

Dear Emmaline — I am sending fireworks. Use the big red one if you need help urgently. Use the white one the night before you plan on making your escape, the golden one an hour before, the green one at time of departure. Fire them right up into the sky above the school — we are keeping watch. Robert tells me you are pestered by large birds of some kind, so I am including some of the yellow shooting stars to keep them away, should you need to. I cannot see that we can provide a workable net or similar safety system for landing purposes, so my suggestion would be that you plan on landing in the sea. I will include the Bellbuckle Patent Life Saver Apparatus, Mark III with our package to you. Yours, Ozymandias Bellbuckle, Professor

Then it was Aunt Lucy's handwriting again.

I expect all will go quite easily from now on. Keep the flying machine under your bed and tell everyone it's an arts and crafts project — they are all the rage, as I understand it. Professor Bellbuckle seems to think you should try to land in the sea, as otherwise you might break both your legs, and then where would you be? See you soon, I hope — love, Aunt Lucy.

P.S. Robert says hello! Lal Singh, too! Toodle-oo!

What a very eccentric letter! Just what she'd expect from Aunt Lucy and this odd scientist person. She wasn't sure about the landing-in-the-sea bit. It was a cold, gray, stormy sea, after all. And she couldn't actually swim. What was this Patent Life Saver Apparatus anyway?

Just then there was a bustle in the corridor behind her. A piercing voice. Miss Scantcommon!

"I am looking for the Cayley girl! I know she is here somewhere!"

"Hide the note," Emmaline told herself. "Not inside your clothes, for they might search you. Where, then?"

Emmaline was half hidden inside a cupboard full of baking powder and suet puddings and Everglue's Spicy Condimental Sauce. Not a promising place for a secret hideaway.

She seized the nearest bottle of sauce, opened it and took a mouthful. Ugh! She took another. Appalling! For even the greatest enthusiasts of Everglue's Sauce don't drink it like water. The manufacturer himself would not have recommended it.

Emmaline tried to slip the folded note into the bottle. But there wasn't enough space without slopping brown sauce everywhere. So she poured a quarter of the bottle on the floor. She slipped the note inside, wiped the top with her apron and put the bottle back on the shelf. Right at the back, where nobody might get to it for weeks.

Then — and this was the cunning part — Emmaline took another bottle of sauce and dropped it onto the flagstone floor from high above her head. It shattered, splattering Everglue's Sauce everywhere. Glass and bits of label were strewn across the pantry.

Since nobody was about to scrape up the remains of the sauce and say, "Hello, there's more than a bottleful here!" her note was safe. Mr. Sherlock Holmes might notice, but he'd never work for such horrible people.

Besides, if Matron was looking for her anyway, being punished for dropping a bottle of Everglue's Spicy Condimental Sauce seemed like a very small addition to the trouble she must already have been in.

The girl decided that tomorrow was the day for escaping. She'd do what all the other girls had tried to do, except that she would manage it. None of the others had done it right. They weren't strong like a mountain goat. They did not have the grip of a monkey. They did not leap like the bounding Pujjikk of Oolistan.

But *she* did.

CHAPTER 23

Someone Else Escapes

Mrs. Wackett was at her most monstrous. She threatened, she postured, she fumed. She shoved her face as close to Emmaline's as she could without actually biting off the girl's nose. The headmistress was like a gargoyle with an ingrown toenail.

"Do you mean to say you know NOTHING of the invasion by those APPALLING Gypsies? Don't lie to me! Don't even think of lying to me!!"

Emmaline wasn't thinking of lying at all. She was keeping her lips sealed tight. Her last meeting with Mrs. Wackett had resulted in her being sent to the Black Tower, but at least, by staying silent she hadn't given anything away.

"Say something, gel! We know you are a mischief-maker and a hooligan and an all-round bad egg! You don't fool me for one moment!" Mrs. Wackett's eyes were huge and blood-shot, unblinking in her glare.

Emmaline sat silent, expressionless. The fact was, Emmaline was no longer nearly as terrified of Mrs. Wackett as she had once been. Mrs. Wackett's power lay in frightening the girls with the threat of "the birds." Emmaline had seen those birds up close. They were very fierce, very dangerous. But she had seen Josie take them on and defeat them. That meant that they were not quite as fierce and dangerous as Mrs. Wackett intended. Whether she, Emmaline, could fight them as her friend had was something she didn't know.

But she felt braver than she had even a day ago.

Mrs. Wackett was going on and on. Most of which was bluster, threats and general noisiness. "Disrespectful chit of a gel — raised by dolts — don't you dare have the nerve to — I'll teach you a lesson, missy!" Emmaline ignored it all. But then the headmistress struck a new note.

"Don't think anyone is impressed that you are spending all your time playing the Ball Game with that hopeless oaf of a girl Josie Pinner."

That phrase smashed through Emmaline's silence. She jumped up and jabbed her finger straight into Mrs. Wackett's wobbling jowls.

"Don't you insult my friend, you ridiculous old battle-ax! You bullying bag of bluster! You nasty, malevolent, ill-natured bag of wind! You venomous, bloated reptile! You jumped-up prison warder! You and your underlings and informers and flying lizards can take a running jump off the tower for all I care!"

This was not what Emmaline had expected to say, or what Mrs. Wackett had expected to hear. Actually, these were the things that Emmaline and Hannah had giggled to one another about the headmistress, never expecting to say them out loud to her or to anyone except one another.

Still, it came out well, with no stammering or forgetting of words. It was a telling off to end all tellings off.

Mrs. Wackett went white. Then her face turned beet red. She yelled, "MATRON!" at the top of her voice as loud as a ship's foghorn.

Miss Scantcommon clamped her scaly white hand on Emmaline's shoulder. Emmaline smiled up at her. "In for a penny, in for a pound," she thought. She might as well continue, since she couldn't get in any worse trouble.

"Miss Scantcommon," said Emmaline in her sweetest voice. "You are a bloodless hag with the soul of a vulture. You are the school ghoul. And all your relatives live in crypts during daylight."

That covered all the really good things that she and Hannah had ever thought up. It was back to the Black Tower. Emmaline thought of biting Matron's arm as they went, but that seemed childish. She didn't want to seem childish.

———

Rubberbones was waiting behind the wall of the grocer's yard as Albert brought the van out. It was painted white and had a big square compartment behind the seat, where the provisions were stored. Albert was on the seat, with room for Mr. Appleburr beside him. Albert gave a wink as he pulled up. Rab adjusted the striped apron and peaked cap that made up his disguise. The door to the shop creaked, and Rab ducked before Old Appleburr stepped out and heaved himself onto the board next to Albert. The van pulled forward as the old chestnut mare began walking. As it reached the curb to turn into the high street, a short, stout woman of middling years dropped her umbrella. The mare was not a young horse, or an excitable horse, so it stopped for the human to clear out of the way.

Rubberbones took the moment to slip from cover and run to the back of the van. The cargo compartment had a door that opened at the rear, and Albert had left the padlock off (actually, he almost always forgot to put it on). In a second or less, the boy was inside with the boxes of provisions and baskets of fruit for St. Grimelda's school. He sat down on a carton of Everglue's Sauce. Albert had already put the package for Emmaline into the back of the van before harnessing the horse. Rab checked it over in case Albert's sense of humor extended to, say, emptying the box and filling it with frogs. He hadn't, which was good.

The journey was bumpy, but nothing Rab could object to. His mind was on the moment when they would reach the school. He knew it had arrived when the van came to a halt. Albert called out in a loud voice, "Morning, Mr. Pinchbeak! Another lovely day we're 'aving!"

Pinchbeak's response could not be heard. Rab thought he was almost certainly mumbling to himself in his discontented, resentful sort of way. The van rolled on.

Albert had told him that the van always stopped just inside the gate while Old Appleburr got out to report to "that thin, tall witch" who was in charge of such things. This was close to where Rab needed to be when it came to slipping into the store sheds, but there was a problem. It was also very close to Pinchbeak's gatekeeper's cabin, and Pinchbeak was a suspicious man. Fortunately, he had some bad habits, or at least behaviors that Matron disapproved of. And Albert liked to help him with his habits, for what he called "a consideration."

Rab could hear Old Appleburr's voice and Matron's, both getting quieter as they walked toward the kitchen doors. He heard Albert's voice, too, in what some people call a "stage whisper" — the tone of a whisper at about three times the volume of a real one. "Mr. Pinchbeak! Got a drop o' rum and some nice shag-cut pipe tobacco for you!"

Pinchbeak snarled back, "Keep thee voice down, y'insolent young whippersnapper, and bring it in 'ere afore anyone sees you." Rab heard Albert jump down and enter the cabin.

Rubberbones leapt out of the van at once with his package, slipping into the cover of the sheds. He put the parcel exactly where he had said he would — in the shed with the green door — and was back to the van in a moment. As he bounded up into the compartment, he heard Albert coming back. "Just made it!" Rab said to himself, wiping his brow in relief.

Albert moved the van closer to the doors of the kitchen pantry and unloaded the supplies. Rab was about to help when Albert reminded him that he wasn't supposed to be there at all. "Just shut up, don't move an' stay out of sight," whispered the grocer's lad. Rab ducked and didn't move a muscle. But the doors were slightly open, so he peeked — as anyone would — and was surprised to see a girl creeping toward him.

The girl — a small thing with wild black hair — tiptoed silently all the way to the van. Looking around warily, she bent down and slid between the wheels. Rubberbones couldn't see her anymore.

"Strange lass!" thought the boy.

Because it had never occurred to Rubberbones that there might be anyone else planning to escape from St. Grimelda's.

———

Emmaline was looking out of the window. It was a different cell and a different view from her last period of "incarceration." This window looked inward over the quad toward the other tower. There wasn't much to see, unless you were interested in the hourly changing of classes or the occasional ratlike scurrying of Pinchbeak.

Emmaline cursed herself silently. She knew that her friends were about to send her the things she needed. At any moment they'd be smuggling a package into the school and hiding it in the shed with the green door, where she could find it and bring it up to the games equipment room. Except now she couldn't, of course, because she'd gone and got herself locked up again.

Stupid! Stupid! Stupid!

Still, it had been nice to say those things to Wackett and Scantcommon!

It had been almost a whole day, as far as Emmaline could guess, since the interview with the headmistress. The chamber had the same hard bed and basic toilet facilities — the best that the Middle Ages had to offer — as her previous tower cell. Matron had brought food and water but had said nothing about what was to happen next. Clearly they had something in store for her. More cleaning out of the cage? More feeding the birds? Maybe this time they were going to feed *her* to the pterodactyls —

That didn't bear thinking about, so she kept looking into the courtyard, hoping for something to distract her thoughts. A horse-drawn delivery van pulled up just inside the gates. It was the grocer's van from the village, the one she had tried to hang onto in order to escape.

Miss Scantcommon strode toward the van.

The grocer climbed out, said something to Miss Scantcommon and followed her back to the main building.

The delivery boy jumped down and went into Pinchbeak's cabin.

Another delivery boy emerged from the back of the van with a large package and disappeared from view behind the storage sheds. Moments later the second delivery boy appeared again, bouncing swiftly back to the van. Emmaline recognized that bouncing step. It was Rubberbones!

The first youth came out of Pinchbeak's cabin and started up the horse with a few words of encouragement. It moved forward to the kitchen doors. The delivery boy spent some time unloading boxes and sacks from the back of the van. Then he began moving things into the doorway, making several trips.

Rab remained out of sight. Suddenly, a girl emerged from cover — she must have been hiding in the shadows of the portico. Someone small and dark-haired. "Good grief!" exclaimed

Emmaline. "It's Purnah!" The royal princess inched silently toward the van and ducked underneath the vehicle.

The delivery boy came back and climbed onto the driver's seat. The grocer appeared from somewhere and got up beside him. Neither seemed to behave unusually.

Miss Scantcommon also came into view. She had her hands on her hips and her eyes on the underside of the van. A narrow, malicious smirk stretched across her face.

Matron was waiting for Princess Purnah to fall off. As soon as the wagon started forward, she would lose her grip, as so many girls before her had done. As Emmaline herself had done.

There were girls around the edge of the quad. They, too, could see what was about to happen. Everyone was deadly quiet.

The wagon started forward toward the gate. Even at the slowest of speeds, there was jolting. Emmaline could see a hand reaching out from under the van, trying to find something firm to grip. Then she could glimpse Purnah's grimacing face beneath the vehicle. Emmaline winced. Surely the princess would fall now!

Suddenly the back door of the van popped open. A hand came out. It reached low and gripped the outstretched hand from under the bed of the wagon.

Rubberbones! His head poked out and his cap fell off while he pulled Princess Purnah into the back of the van as it passed through the gates. Miss Scantcommon goggled in astonishment. Rab waved at Matron and pulled the van door shut.

A massive cheer went up from all around the quad.

Nothing like this had ever happened before. Emmaline felt a rush of joy, of pride — and a bit of revenge. It was almost worth being a prisoner in a tower for moments like this! Almost, but not quite.

What would happen next?

CHAPTER 24

The Trilocopede

"I is Purnah, Royal Princess of Chiligrit!" announced the wild-haired girl. She seemed excited, her bright eyes gleaming. Rab put his finger to his lips in the universal sign for "hush." Beyond the partition two voices were arguing.

"Albert, steady on a bit. You're driving too fast!"

"Oh, no, Mr. Appleburr. The 'orse likes a bit of a trot now and then. And we're late for delivery at Wisteria Manor. You know 'ow the 'ousekeeper is there — proper old dragon!"

"Don't be disrespectful to your elders, Albert. Did you hear a lot of noise when we were leaving the school?"

"No, Mr. Appleburr. Must've been the wind."

"I am certain I heard a lot of girls shouting."

"Probably cheering, Mr. Appleburr. Probably just heard they'd been given a half holiday or something."

Rubberbones had to think. Albert had told him that they had one more delivery to make before returning to the village. If Old Appleburr became suspicious, Rab was to climb quietly out at Wisteria Manor and make his way back through the woods to Fishwick. About two miles, Rab guessed. But now he had an escaped schoolgirl with him and surely there'd be folk looking for her. What to do?

He peered through a crack in the door and saw something racing down the road from the school. Pursuit. They were after him. Her. Them.

Emmaline heard voices on the steps outside her cell and footsteps on the stairs. It was Matron and Mrs. Wackett running up to the pterodactyls' coop; they seemed to be quarrelling over the incident in the quad.

"— you were just standing there watching!"

"— nothing like that ever happened before!"

"— get the blasted trilocopede, then —"

"— heck of a risk letting the birds loose in the daytime."

"— what choice do we have?"

"— heck to pay if anyone sees them and word gets out!"

"— heck of a price if we don't, though!"

Emmaline felt a thrill of excitement hearing the two teachers cursing away like sailors. They were in a panic and arguing about what to do. Emmaline looked out the window again. The girls had all been ushered to their classrooms. Miss Sharpelbow was alone in the quad, seated on the saddle of the strangest vehicle Emmaline had ever seen. What was that bizarre contraption? It was — it had to be — "the blasted trilocopede."

The trilocopede was to the tricycle what the lion is to a tabby cat. It had two huge wheels like the front wheel on a penny-farthing bicycle with a small single wheel at the back. It had two high saddles and a trumpetlike horn mounted on the handlebars that could be sounded by a rubber bulb the size of a football. It was black and shiny and looked very fast indeed.

Miss Scantcommon appeared within moments, mounting the other saddle in a single motion. The two teachers began to pedal furiously. The trilocopede started forward, picking up speed. An enormous blast, like that of a foghorn, erupted from it. Then it vanished through the gates. Above the walls, Emmaline spotted two ominous shapes gliding against the sun. So, they had released the pterodactyls. They were serious about it. Nobody escapes from St. Grimelda's.

The grocer's van was going at a trot, which was a tremendous surprise for the old horse, who had more or less forgotten how to move at more than a sluggish walk. It was a surprise for the grocer too — Rubberbones could hear him through the wall shouting at Albert.

"Slow down, you young fool! What's got into you?"

Albert seemed to be gritting his teeth as he shouted back. "About to rain. Running late — I think your watch might have stopped. Horse needs the exercise." The blare of a mighty horn sounded behind them. Rab peered again out through the crack in the door.

A shape was barreling down the road toward them at astounding speed. He had no idea what it was. It was a towering conveyance with massive wheels, making a succession of blasts like a tugboat with a drunken captain. He had no doubt that the two figures riding on top were from St. Grimelda's.

Just as frightening — if not more — were the shapes that Rab made out among the clouds. It was those birds again. They were circling, scouting. Rubberbones had no idea whether they knew how to follow a scent, like hounds, or if they were like birds of prey looking for, well, prey. His last encounter with the birds had been terrifying, and Rab was not a boy who terrified easily. Unfriendly dogs, burly footballers, farmers with sticks — those were the things he was used to. The leathery birds, however, were, as he put it, "summat else."

Then Rab saw a Gypsy caravan poking out into the road, back-end first. There was no horse in the traces. It was being pushed into the road by several people in traditional Romany costume and a large Sikh.

"Champion!" exclaimed Rubberbones to Princess Purnah. The princess answered in a flurry of words that Rab didn't

understand at all. From the other side of the wooden partition, Old Appleburr said, "Albert! There's something inside the van!" Rubberbones shut up and gestured for Purnah to do the same. Albert, sounding desperate, said "Mice, Mr. Appleburr. Bloomin' things get everywhere."

The trilocopede raced on, huge wheels bounding in the ruts of the lane. The horn was honking madly. The Gypsy wagon rolled out farther into the pathway. Surely they would collide!

Rubberbones had never seen anything like the tall, squawk-ing trilocopede (he'd no idea it was called that), but he had seen all sorts of bicycles. He'd ridden on a cousin's second-hand penny-farthing once. They could go fast and were terrific once you got them going. If you fell off, it was from very high up, and straight over the handlebars, so the bike could run over you as you landed. This was great fun if you were a rubber boy, but not if you weren't. Rab's cousin had broken his arm, cut his face and cried, which is humiliating when you are thirteen. So Rab knew that a smash-up would be a bad thing, even if the injured were all teachers.

But there was no smash-up. As the Gypsy band pushed the wagon into the road, the trilocopede veered crazily onto one side. It leaped into the air and landed beyond the caravan. It hooted angrily and was coming on again. Rab couldn't believe it. Things were bad, because the pursuers were still on his tail, but it was champion, just the same. One day he'd get a machine just like it.

Just then the birds came down like a clap of thunder, screaming like banshees, claws extended. They swooped toward the grocer's van. Princess Purnah let out a blood-curdling scream (Albert couldn't very well say *this* was a mouse among the provisions) and hurled herself as far back into the van as she could. Rab hauled the door shut, and there was a tearing noise as talons ripped across the roof.

"Mice, Albert? Mice!" called a very shaky voice from the front seat.

Rubberbones looked up. There was a deep gash in the roof. The back door flapped open, and he saw that the van had entered a natural tunnel where the trees folded over the road in a canopy of branches. The birds must have sheered off to avoid the trees. Which was good, for now. But they had trouble enough, for the trilocopede was bearing down on them at astonishing speed.

Suddenly Princess Purnah popped up beside him, eyes ablaze with fury and her voice raised in what sounded like a curse. A missile flew from her right hand. It sped with tremendous force, and the aim was true.

There was a burst of white mist. Miss Scantcommon swayed in the saddle, clutching her head. Her hat fell off. Her face was white. Her clothes were white.

Princess Purnah threw another bag of flour. This one caught the right wheel, scattering another fog of white across Miss Sharpelbow. Rubberbones was rummaging through the provisions himself. A tin of treacle, a smoked ham, a bottle of olive oil. There was lard, too, and butter — good, slippery stuff. Rubberbones brought a pound of butter up to the edge of the jolting van, ripped off the wrapper and dropped it onto the road. Princess Purnah did the same with a block of lard. The trilocopede's left wheel caught the lard cleanly on its iron tire and ran right over it. The conveyance skidded sharply to the left, tipping toward the ditch. Miss Scantcommon looked as if she would fall into the hedge. Her colleague leaned to the right, for balance and the machine bounced back upright. It had fallen behind thirty feet now. This was good, though Princess Purnah wasted a perfectly good tin of kippers trying to hit Matron at such a distance.

The grocer's van was completely out of control. The horse had panicked — as any sensible animal who had seen two monsters pass overhead might do — and was galloping in a geriatric fashion. The van flung from side to side. Albert and

Old Appleburr had stopped arguing because they were desperately trying to get the horse under control. The path ran downhill toward Wisteria Manor, where the housekeeper would be awaiting the provisions that two small figures were busy throwing out all over the roadway.

Princess Purnah found the olive oil. This time she did not throw the bottle at Matron's head. Instead, she opened it and, leaning far forward, shook the oil across the lane in a trail of slippery golden liquid. Rubberbones grinned.

The trilocopede hit the oiled patches with both wheels at once, locking their motion into a vast skid sideways into the ditch. The machine bounced from the hedge back into the road to slam into the grocer's van, which had finally been pulled from a crazed gallop to an exhausted stagger by means of Albert's tugging and the horse's advanced age.

There was an almighty smash. Rubberbones saw it coming, mouth agape as the huge contraption thundered down on the rattling wreck of the grocer's van. He saw one of the tall females fly overhead while the other pitched sideways into a hedge. Then the wooden panels of the van crumpled into splinters, and something hit him on the head.

Everything went black.

CHAPTER 25

The Eccentric Colonel

"Ugh!" mumbled Rubberbones. "Ouch." It hurt when he tried to move. This was a novel feeling for him, being a rubber boy. His bones didn't break but, still, he thought, it flippin' well *'urt*.

"You was hit severishly on the head by flying tinnage of peas. Then van fell over. You was throwed out through the roof — making a bigling hole in roof than was previously to your passage. Ha! Porok! Then you hits a most substantial oak tree and falls in a puddle. How I laughs! Tringg! Then I drags you by your leglings to this very nice hawthorn bush, which is a bit spiky, but convenient. Please be quiet, now."

It was a small voice with an odd accent. A bit posh, but foreign. A bit like somebody who could understand English words but wasn't used to saying them. Rab peered blearily up to see the girl. She was wiry and wild-looking, her uniform rumpled and ripped. She had pigtails that swung as she waved a finger at Rubberbones's face. Rab thought that her teeth, which flashed as she spoke, were probably very sharp.

"There is much confusing over there." Purnah pointed fiercely to the road, where Rab could barely make out the crushed remains of the van and the trilocopede jammed together. He heard raised voices: Albert explaining, Old Appleburr complaining and shrill females making angry threats. Purnah had no time to watch the scene. "We must removal ourselves from vicinity before deaths is upon us. Quickish! Hrripp!"

She pulled Rab to his feet, tugging him by the arm through the forest. Autumn was turning the leaves to gold and rusty red. The trees gave cover from pursuers.

"The foul Scantcommon and her noisy teacherly friend will chasings, if they is not baddish injured by collision. Gollop! Oh, how I hopes they is maimed within inches of their cruel lives!"

The rubber boy and the wild princess ran, sometimes slipping on wet leaves, down into the valley. They were close to the edge of the forest; an open field where hay had been cut lay ahead. Purnah burst from cover, spurting forward across the pasture. "Run, Errand Boy, run! Glekk! We must make hastings away from here!"

Errand Boy, as he was not used to being called, limped behind. Had he really been thrown through the roof of the grocer's van? he wondered. He'd never felt so banged up. At least, not since he fell off the tower of the old priory at Grumpleby when he was ten; that had hurt, but it was near thirty feet onto flagstones.

They ran across the open ground. Rubberbones didn't see the bird at all until it was upon them. It came from behind, taking Princess Purnah by surprise. It was far bigger than she was, and swooped swiftly, its talons out. Thinking fast, she fell face forward as the creature tore the schoolgirl hat from her head. The beast shrieked in frustration. Then it attacked again, seized Purnah around the middle and began lifting her into the air.

Rab raced forward, gritting his teeth in pain. He had no weapon, no slingshot, no tin of peas. He was mortally afraid of the monstrous beings that even he knew were not birds. But he knew he had to save Purnah from being torn to shreds. (It was only good manners, and anyway his gran would expect him to.) So he grabbed the horrible thing by what might have been its ankles, and tugged. The thing squawked. Rab dug his heels in and held on. Princess Purnah, gripped by evil-looking talons, screamed. The beast flapped its mas-sive leathery wings. But it could not lift the weight of both children. It couldn't reach down to bite — though it was trying hard, and didn't seem fussy about what it ate — so it fluttered, like a sinister giant bat. Rubberbones was as anxious as anyone to avoid being a morning snack for a flying horror. He held on as if it were the annual football match and the monster had turned out for the Upper Owlthwaite team in a surprising (and completely unfair) selection.

"Those cheats from Upper Owlthwaite would do something like that, given half a chance," he declared.

"Wotting the heckish you on abouts?" demanded Purnah, clamped in the monster's grip. "Is you maddish?"

Things looked bad. Things looked worse than bad. Things looked terrible.

BANG! The sound was deafening. BANG! Again. Then there was a jolt; the bird lurched in the air, and Princess Purnah fell from its talons. The flying monster staggered sideways, and Rab let go as he was pulled off his feet. The big wings flapped (actually just one wing flapped, the other hung weakly), and the creature retreated across the field and into the trees. Its partner wheeled above the wood, emitting a horrid shriek. There was another bang, and it vanished from view.

"Are you two kiddies all right?" asked a kindly voice. Rab looked up. He wasn't sure he liked being called a "kiddie," as he was twelve and a quarter, but this was no time to worry about that sort of thing. The speaker was an elderly man in country tweeds with a pith helmet and sensible shoes. He broke open his shotgun and slipped in a cartridge. He wore disturbingly thick glasses for a man with a gun.

"Big dashed bird, what? Seen 'em around these parts, though never had a chance to pot at one 'til now. Thought it must be some kind of crow. Never seen a crow try to pick up children before!"

Rubberbones was about to say that the monstrous creature looked nothing at all like a crow (it was like comparing a rat to a crocodile). But the man was speaking, and it was rude to interrupt a grown-up, especially when the grown-up in question was clearly a gentleman. (Rab's gran would have told him to stand up straight, doff his cap and address him as "sir.") Also, he was armed with a loaded shotgun.

Rab picked his cap up off the ground, flourished it and grinned like an idiot, which was as close to politeness as he could manage. It had been a difficult morning for him. Purnah had rolled into the long grass. She popped up, smiling, grass in her hair, as if she'd been expecting to be rescued at any moment.

"Pleased to meet you both! Grimble-Boare's the name! Eleventh Hussars, y'know, Waterloo and Balaclava! Well, not Waterloo — eighty years ago — far too young! But Charge of the Light Brigade and all and all. I was a young whippersnapper then myself, of course! Come in and have a spot of lunch!"

Princess Purnah stood up very gingerly. Her uniform was ripped to shreds. This was not revealing, or indecent, since there were so many garments, but Rubberbones looked away in embarrassment. She looked like a pantomime witch who had been attacked by a threshing machine. But she did not seem hurt.

"Corsets!" she announced, pointing at her undergarments. "Whalebone corsets. Like armor!"

"Jolly good!" said Colonel Grimble-Boare. (It was obvious he was a colonel; he didn't have to say so.) "Shall we have a quick dekko into the woods to see if that crow is still there? Hate to leave a wounded bird to suffer."

Both Rubberbones and the princess shook their heads.

The colonel made a snorting sound. "Probably not wise. I only loaded with light shot for partridges. Probably not enough to really hurt a crow of that size. Dashed biggun, doncha think?"

So, as he burbled on about crows that tried to attack children ("... one to tell 'em at the Cavalry Club in Piccadilly next time I'm in London, quite amazin', remember a time in Sumatra — or was it Burma?..."), Rubberbones and Princess Purnah followed him anxiously across the field to a very large house — and climbed in through the French windows.

Emmaline had been in the tower room for hours. Since Matron and the games mistress had left in that very odd tricyclelike contraption, everything was quiet. Very quiet indeed, as if the whole school was being kept in some kind of lockup. Still, she kept looking out of the window. Then she saw it — a single figure creeping toward the storage buildings close to the gateway. It was a schoolgirl, sneaking into the shed with the green roof. A few moments later she came out again, carrying a large package and looking around shiftily.

"My parcel from Aunt Lucy!" cried Emmaline.

Things weren't looking good.

The colonel was a charming host. He brought the two young-sters into what Rab thought might be called a "morning room," and rang for tea and cakes and jam and jellies. Colonel Grimble-Boare had a sweet tooth; at his advanced age he could have anything he liked for lunch.

"And lots of chocolate, too," he instructed the long-faced housekeeper. "These young people need their strength built up."

The housekeeper grumbled something about the grocer's delivery being late and not much to be found in the pantry. But the colonel was interested only in his young visitors. A bell rang, and the woman marched toward the door.

"Let me see. A young lady from the mysterious East? And a local lad? Not eloping, are we?" he added with a wink.

"Goodness, no! Horrokk!" replied Purnah. "I is princess in my homeland, the land of Chiligrit, escaping from wicked captivity. This servant is errand boy only." She waved at Rab with a dismissive gesture.

Rubberbones glared at her. This strange schoolgirl might very well be a princess, but he wasn't anybody's servant, or an errand boy. Well, maybe he was Miss Aunt Lucy's, but she never referred to him that way. He glared again. "I am not an errand boy. I am a pioneer aviator!" He'd heard Emmaline use that term.

"You *are* dressed as an errand boy," pointed out Colonel Grimble-Boare.

"A scruffy one," added Princess Purnah, who was clearly offended by this turn in the conversation. "Pillik!"

Before Rubberbones could explain that he was, in fact, a pioneer aviator who doubled as an errand boy purely as a form of disguise, the housekeeper returned. She had a grim expression on her face.

"Grocer's delivery is off, sir. Some kind of accident. All the supplies strewn across the road. Mr. Appleburr's babbling some nonsense about being attacked. I told him to stop making excuses and bring us the right order this afternoon. Says his van has been wrecked. 'Stop your sniveling,' I says. Oh, and there are two ladies from the girls' school who want to see you. I told them to wait in the parlor. Dreadfully filthy, too, if you don't mind me saying. Standards are falling everywhere."

"Porok!" muttered Purnah. She looked back at the French windows to check her escape route.

"Thank you, Mrs. Gripewell," said the colonel. "Please inform the ladies that I will be with them shortly. Offer them tea, if we still have some. And please do NOT mention that I have company at this time."

The housekeeper grunted to indicate that she had no intention of revealing anything to the bedraggled schoolmistresses, and left the room.

The colonel leaned forward. "Can I assume that these are the people you are escaping from?"

Purnah and Rab started in surprise, then both nodded mutely at the old man.

"I will delay them while you leave through those windows. Strategy, what! Across the field, then through Peel's wood to a stile. There's a narrow lane there to the village. Keep close to the hedge. Duck if you hear anything. Stay quiet, and you'll be fine."

Both youngsters murmured their thanks, refusing an offer of revolvers or a sword. The princess wanted the sword (and an ancient blunderbuss hanging over the hearth), but Rab shook his head.

"Probably not such a good idea," sighed the colonel. "Toodle-oo!"

Emmaline heard the school gates clanking open. When she rushed to the window, she saw something she certainly didn't expect. Miss Sharpelbow and Matron trudged slowly through, pushing the wrecked trilocopede. It had lost a saddle and a set of handlebars, and one big wheel was bent crazily. The two women proceeded across the quad with a failed attempt at dignity, glaring at a girl who sniggered at them. They were both limping and covered in mud, with patches of something white over their faces and clothes. Both had lost their hats, and there was a massive rip down Matron's coat. Emmaline particularly enjoyed the white streak on Miss Sharpelbow's hair, which made her look like a giant badger.

Emmaline smiled to see the teachers returning like tramps. She needed a bit of entertainment. But what could it all mean?

CHAPTER 26

Glekk! Porok!

Rubberbones and Princess Purnah reached the narrow lane and began the walk down toward the village. They kept close to the hedge and listened carefully for anything following them. Could the two teachers have stolen a donkey or commandeered a hay cart or found some other way of keeping up the hot pursuit?

As they slunk along, Princess Purnah spoke. "I am sorry I believings you to be servant, Errand Boy. What is this 'aviator' thing of which you speakish?"

"Er ... I fly," said Rubberbones.

"Phfew! Glekk! You are a boy. You do not fly!"

"I do too!" insisted Rab hotly. "I fly in a sort of big kite."

"Klimgil! Porok! What kite be this? I believes you tell lies." Princess Purnah seemed scornful at the idea that Rab could really fly.

"It's true, I swear. Miss Emmaline makes flying machines. We fly 'em off roofs and church towers."

"Emmaline? Is girl in my school called Emmaline." Purnah's eyes flashed with a gleam of interest.

"That's the one. I'm going to help 'er get out of there."

"Flizgit! So that is why you is lurking suspiciously in the grocer's njebet?"

Rab had to think about this. The princess used a lot of words that were not English, and Rab only knew English words, and mostly just those that people used in Lower Owlthwaite. Miss Em and her aunt talked a bit posh, and the professor said some quite unusual things, but none of them talked about "njebets" or exclaimed "Porok!" He nodded. Nods can take you a long way.

"Emmaline Cayley" — the princess pronounced it "Ki-lee" — "she always in trouble with the guards. Escape tries. Beatings with sticks. Feeding the birds."

"Beatings! Feeding them birds!" exclaimed Rubberbones.

Purnah gestured him to hush. "Oh yess. Most badling girl. Always locked up in the Black Tower."

Rab was about to ask more when the sound of a wagon came from around the bend in the lane. Both youngsters ducked into the ditch. Rab cursed himself for making so much noise. The hoofbeats slowed, then stopped.

"Come on out. Get inside."

"Glekk!" squealed Princess Purnah.

But Rubberbones knew the voice. It was the Gypsy chief, the Romany lord that everyone called Sid. (Rab had noticed that Sid always seemed to pop up at just the right moment.)

Everything was all right with the world. Except for the bit about Emmaline feeding the birds, and the guards and the beatings.

------◈------

Emmaline could hear the voices outside her cell. It was Matron and the horrid Pinchbeak. Checking to see if the birds had returned. Miss Scantcommon was talking.

"Neither of our birds has come back," she said anxiously. "I knew it was a bad idea to send them out in daylight. They aren't used to it. Watch for them, Pinchbeak. I hope neither of them has been hurt in any way."

Odd. Matron sounded ... attached. As if it was her pet canary that had been allowed to fly out of an open window.

"Shouldn't worry," said Pinchbeak. "They are ruddy big, mean varmints. I ain't never seen the like meself. Where did the school get 'em, anyway?"

"That's not for you to ask, Pinchbeak. Suffice to say, there have been birds at St. Grimelda's since the founding of the school. They've been our most effective means of keeping ill-behaved young girls in line. That's all you need to know."

Pinchbeak made a grunting sound. "What about the Cayley girl, then?"

"Clearly, we were mistaken about her involvement in recent events. It was Princess Purnah, of all people, who was plotting to escape. Cayley was very rude to the head and myself, of course, but we can manage that sort of behavior. Let her out and we'll administer appropriate punishment."

Emmaline stayed quiet. What was going on? The birds hadn't come back, and Scantcommon was worried about what had happened. And somehow Princess Purnah's escape had let Emmaline off the hook. Well, what was the old proverb —

"never look a gift horse in the mouth"? She was not about to. The key turned in the lock.

"All right, Miss Cayley," said Matron in her steeliest tone. "I believe you are late for Latin. Run along. Oh, and you'll be on pots and pans until, mmm, the end of the century. And that's just the start of your punishment! Don't think you'll get off this easily next time, my gel!"

Emmaline found it much easier than ever before to say, "Thank you, Matron."

―――――

They were gathered at Professor Bellbuckle's cottage. "They" meaning Aunt Lucy and Lal Singh, the professor, Rubberbones, Princess Purnah and their Gypsy friends. Everyone acted as if it was quite natural for an escaped foreign princess to be seated on the sofa in a shredded school uniform eating chocolate cake. Stanley was there, too, bounding around in unrestrained fashion. Rubberbones was happy that his scheme to hide the parcel had worked well, and everyone had shaken his hand in congratulation. Aunt Lucy had made him a special turnip-and-earwig pie to celebrate. Still, they were a long way from releasing Emmaline. His worries hadn't gone away.

"It's a step forward," said Aunt Lucy. "Don't fret so." But Rab could tell that she was uneasy herself.

The Gypsies had decided that it was time to depart.

"We wanted to stay with you until Miss Emmaline had everything she needs to make her escape," explained Sid. "But today's business will have the coppers out seeking yon princess, and a band of Gypsies is always the first thing they'll hold up. So we'd best be on our way now. We'll see you again." He smiled warmly and slapped Rab on the back so hard that the lad almost fell over. "And charmed to meet you, your Royal Majesty!"

Her Royal Majesty had crammed her mouth full of chocolate icing, so she waved a sticky hand.

"And I shall be sure to find out what is going on with you at all times," said Madame ZaZa in her most mystical voice.

"You mean with the crystal ball and the tea leaves?" asked Rab excitedly.

"Well, mostly by gossip. We Romany like to keep up with the news. But the crystal ball is useful, too."

Rab knew that Rollo was eager to be off with his pals to sell horses (horses he didn't actually own). Also, Rollo did not want to meet Albert again. He thought there was every chance that Albert might blame him for the escape of Princess Purnah. He definitely thought that Albert might be in a bad mood.

After the caravan had departed, with much waving and a parting gift on both sides (mushroom marmalade from Aunt Lucy and yet more chocolate cake from Madame ZaZa), everyone sat down in the parlor to talk. Everyone except Stanley, who bounded around from room to room.

Aunt Lucy turned to Princess Purnah. "Tell us about yourself, dear. I hear you are a princess. That must be nice."

Even Rubberbones knew that being held prisoner and then attacked by flying monsters was not really "nice." The princess didn't object, though.

"Excuse my speakage." Purnah sat upright, as if she was holding court, and handled her teacup exactly as Miss Silverspoon had shown her. She had chocolate all over her cheeks and nose. "I only learn English from listening to other girls at horrid, horrid school. I am there three years, never say anything, never act like I understand anything, except when people shouts at me. Is pretending stupid, as is best way of avoiding assassinationing. I learns that from my wicked cousins. English people think shouting makes language understood to foreign peoples. Also speaking slow like you are idiot. This helpful, as sometimes I forgets I not supposed to understand language, but nobody ever notice. School-teachers not seem to care if I learn anything. Just be quiet girl and causing no difficulties."

"That's terrible!" exclaimed Aunt Lucy.

"Abominable treatment!" agreed Professor Bellbuckle.

"Blinkin' unfair!" Rab chimed in.

Stanley thought it was wrong, too, and ran round with a sock in his mouth to show his agreement. Lal Singh remained silent, which usually meant he was concentrating.

Questions came tumbling out of Aunt Lucy. "Where are you from? What were you doing at that school? Where were you escaping to?"

Princess Purnah told her story in bits of English with many hand gestures and proclamations of things like "porok!" and "glekk!" to add color and excitement.

"I am honored daughter of esteemed, though much deceased, Mir — which is ruler — of Chiligrit, which lie above Yargarwar and below Rootitooty, near the horrible Hoolgars and despicable Deepos, far north-east-west of India and under the high Frizzibuttok Mountains. In my country is many enemies from outside and inside also, like my father's cousin, Sneekidivil, and my uncle, Bakistabbo. When I am ten there is rebellings by the ungrateful mountain people against my beloved father. When he went out smitings them righteously and cutting off heads as a good ruler must, he was — what is word? — betrayaled by Sneekidivil and Bakistabbo. They killing my father most treasonably, with help of agents of evil-yet-faraway Zarr of Roozha. I have older brother and three sisters, all get thrown in dungeons. Possibly murdered, or not. I escapes with help of British 'resident' — is like an advice-person — and sent to India. They deciding what do with me. English lady say, 'I know excellent school for girls!' I say to her, 'Grobikk Pish!!' They send me here with nice English lady. Not same as first English lady. School tell her I be fine now, don't come back, don't write. Liars! Liars! Glekk! Oloba!"

"You mean the British government of India sent you to St. Grimelda's?" asked Professor Bellbuckle.

"Yes! Send me in company of nice lady. But I hear from her no more. Not allowed write. I write in my language, a littlish. Is Chiligriti, good language, not barbarous like Hoolgars and Deepos is speaking. Pish! Nobody in England write Chiligriti or speak it."

Lal Singh leaned forward and addressed the girl in a stream of an unknown tongue. Princess Purnah's eyes grew big, and she replied in the same language.

"Useful fella, that one," observed the professor to Aunt Lucy. "Always full of surprises." Stanley barked in full agreement.

Aunt Lucy poured a pot of her best nettle tea all round.

"Tell me, dear, all about this school you escaped from. We will look after you, and make sure nobody harms you, and get you back to your home and loved ones if it can be done. But we also need to help my niece Emmaline get out of that place, so anything you can tell us is welcome. Anything and everything, please."

Rab felt even more nervous than he had before. He could see the unease in Aunt Lucy's face, and even Lal Singh seemed worried. What sort of school was this?

CHAPTER 27

Bats? Crocodiles? Automatons?

The first thing that Emmaline did, once she had a few moments to herself, was to seek out Josie. This was harder to do than usual because the school was on a severe restriction in which no outdoor activities were allowed. This was obviously the result of Purnah's escape (which everyone knew about), but Emmaline suspected that with the pterodactyls loose, Mrs. Wackett was also concerned about her pupils being attacked or eaten if the birds returned empty-handed and hungry. (That'd be hard to explain to parents.) Two girls were reprimanded in Latin class for simply looking out of the window. There was no Ball Game. Teachers walked the girls between classes in strict silence. And Emmaline's chore of doing the pots and pans for the whole school after dinner — a monstrous task by any reckoning — put her in the scullery for two hours. That was where Josie (in charge of putting the plates and cups away) found her first.

"What happened in the tower?" whispered Josie. Madame De Gauloise, the French teacher, was in charge of supervising chores this evening, and she had a habit of sneaking out into the back courtyard every so often that Emmaline found helpful. She always reeked of cigarettes when she returned, and you could smell the tobacco before she came through the door.

"Not much at all. They just kept me there. I overheard

some conversations, though. The birds have gone out and not come back."

"Flippin' 'eck!" replied Josie, taken aback. "They never, ever, let 'em out in the daytime. Somebody might see 'em, and the word would get out. There'd be people from the government and scientists and all askin' questions."

"They sent the pterodactyls after Princess Purnah. They were in a real tizzy, I can tell you," said Emmaline in a hushed voice.

"Course they were. Nobody expected her to actually get out. Girls try that stunt all the time. Never works. Didn't work for you. Didn't work for me when I tried it — first month I got here."

"Well, it worked today. That was my friend Robert who helped her into the grocer's van."

"Give over! The little flying lad?"

"He's sharp for twelve. He surprised me, too, today. Probably surprised Purnah most of all. But listen," Emmaline continued. "I've got some horrible news! He brought a package of things for the kite and hid it in one of the sheds by Pinchbeak's cabin. I saw a girl sneak out with it a bit later. Someone has stolen everything we need to make the kite into a proper flyer!"

Just then there was the sound of footsteps in the passage-way. Madame De Gauloise was returning. "Shh!" whispered Josie. "The equipment room. After lights-out."

Emmaline saw a figure out of the corner of her eye. It was not the French schoolmistress. There was no whiff of tobacco. It was one of the two identical twins, Petronella or perhaps the other one, staring straight at her, like a hawk viewing a juicy dormouse.

Professor Bellbuckle was hard at work in his laboratory. Rubberbones had become his assistant by simply hanging around. Stanley was assisting as well; while Rab handed the professor strange tools from the racks on the wall, the dog busily pulled brass widgets and leather tubes onto the floor.

Rab liked to use the Bellbuckle Patent Telephonic Tubular Vocalgraphic Communicators that connected each room of the cottage and the professor's shed. This was a lot like something called the "telephone," patented back in 1876 by Alexander Graham Bell. The professor ignored Bell's invention, feeling that his own was vastly superior. His device featured clockwork parts and a little bit of gunpowder. (The professor liked clockwork and gunpowder.) It was not connected to the outside world, however, owing to the outside world's odd preference for using the system that already worked.

The device had a bell, which sounded like a singing mouse. It went off. All the lights in the house (which were homemade electric bulbs operated by a windmill with a big rubber band and paper sails) went out. A few seconds later, the lights flashed back on.

"Bellbuckle here. Oh, right, yes, who else would it be? Coffee, Lucy? Why, I do believe I'd like some. Not so much cinnamon and sardine in it this time, if you don't mind. All right, ma'am, maybe just a little sardine."

The professor, however, was a man who could put other work aside.

"Our concern right now is to be ready when Miss Emmaline makes her escape. We need a boat, and some means of fending off those beasts you told me about. From your description of these creatures I think it's unlikely they are actual birds. I believe there are two possibilities. The first is that the so-called birds are the result of some form of cross-breeding between the larger sort of bat and a crocodile or similar carnivorous amphibian —"

"Cor!" said Rubberbones. "Half-bat, half-crocodile. That'd be champion!"

Professor Bellbuckle chuckled. "No doubt it would, but that's the lesser of the two possibilities. More likely, in my opinion, is that the 'birds' are mechanical automata created by an advanced science beyond our current understanding. I assume they are made of a light metal frame covered in a waterproof skin and obey messages sent by radiophonic transmission from that tower." He pointed in the direction of St. Grimelda's.

"You mean they aren't real?" asked Rubberbones in amazement.

"Gosh, no, my boy. They are infernal devices, invented by an evil genius with incredible engineering abilities. The noises you have told me about are clearly the signals that operate their working systems. Most ingenious."

"Amazin'! Champion!"

"We will therefore need to come up with some device of our own — a weapon, perhaps, or something to intercept the radiophonic waves that control these machines. A sound transmitter with high-pitched shrieking, maybe, or the kind of piercing sound that only a dog can hear. Stanley could help with that."

Stanley looked up, shaking his rump with enthusiasm.

The bell rang again. This time the voice on the other end belonged to Princess Purnah, who liked the strange device.

"Greetings, Professor Bellbuckle, Errand Boy and small dog. I am bringing traylings of coffee and confectionable items across from kitching. Please opens door when I arrives as all my hands are containing whole tray."

The professor laughed and said he would.

Suddenly Stanley's ears pricked up. Rab could hear what he assumed was the clinking of china on a tray. Then a chittering noise, like some kind of wild creature, and the crash of cups.

"Glekk! Usamu! Virtado Tog!" shouted Princess Purnah.

There was a sound like the beating of wings.

The professor nearly tore the door from its hinges. Rubberbones was behind him, cannoning through the doorway into the yard. Stanley barked and bounded. It was all too late. Above them, Princess Purnah was waving her legs and beating her fists against the scaly hide of the great flying beast. "Porok!" she shouted and tried to bite its feet. The second flying creature spun around overhead. They wheeled over the rooftop as the princess yelled and thrashed in the talons of the pterodactyl. Then they were gone.

Rubberbones yelled helplessly, throwing stones from the pathway. Stanley barked without ceasing. Professor Bellbuckle just stood and watched, slack-jawed, as the monstrous things flew away.

"Son. That weren't no automaton. Nor was it an experimental bat-crocodile crossbreed. That was something much stranger. That was something as ought to have been dead these past sixty million years."

———

Emmaline tiptoed through the darkened dormitory, picking her way between the gently snoring bodies of her classmates. She was becoming good at these nighttime excursions. She passed through the doorway into the hall and up the stairs toward the equipment room. There was a long window at the landing where the stairs wound upward. She looked out. The moon was up, and the sky was light with twinkling stars. Two shapes were crossing the heavens from the south. Batlike shapes, flapping toward the Black Tower. One of them had something hanging limply from its claws. It was carrying something. Actually, carrying some*one*.

The birds had returned.

CHAPTER 28

A Well-Wisher

The door opened and Josie, touching a finger to her lips, ushered Emmaline inside.

"Them birds are back," she whispered. "They got Princess Purnah, I 'spect."

"One of them was carrying somebody. Or some *body*," Emmaline replied, shuddering at the thought.

"I can't say for certain, but I believe they're like those hunters' dogs that just fetch ducks. They prob'ly won't have harmed her."

"What if it's someone else they've caught?" worried Emmaline, thinking about Rubberbones. "What if the creatures have attacked and captured Rab or someone from the village? There'd be trouble then, wouldn't there?"

"I s'pose. But I think the birds are like dogs in another way, too. You set 'em on a smell — a bit of clothing or some-such — and they go after it. Otherwise they'd just attack anyone they came across."

"But you're sure that Purnah will be unharmed?" Emmaline asked anxiously.

Josie looked uneasy. "No. Not sure at all."

Rubberbones was furious. He couldn't believe that here at Professor Bellbuckle's laboratory, with chocolate cake and

Miss Aunt Lucy's horrible sardine-flavored coffee and friends all around, the terrible birds had snatched Princess Purnah. Just like that. The professor felt the same. He was mumbling something about building a piece of artillery that could fire high into the air.

Aunt Lucy appeared more calm — and practical. "Well, not a lot to be done right now," she said, sweeping up the remains of the tea service. "I shall write a strongly worded letter to the India Office about the princess being held against her wishes at that appalling school and see if she has any relatives or guardians who might help. I shan't mention those horrible birds — pterodactyls, you say? Fancy that ... anyway, it doesn't do any good to appear to be a lunatic in the eyes of authority. Meanwhile, I suppose we could chase her blindly across the moors in the dark, following as best as we can, but my guess is that those beasts are trained to take their prey back to that wicked school. Either that or eat her in some craggy nest somewhere."

"Eat her!!" shouted Rab, appalled.

"I'll be gosh-darned if I permit that sweet young thing to become those durned varmints' vittles!" swore the professor.

"All well and good," continued Aunt Lucy, "but we must look at the facts straight on. If she's eaten, she's eaten. If not, that's to the good. If she's taken to the school, well, perhaps she'll talk to Emmaline and they can help each other. Once the wounds heal, of course."

This put Rubberbones and the professor to cursing once more, blaming themselves for everything and generally making a lot of noise.

"Men!" said Aunt Lucy, mostly to herself. "Can't face plain facts without making a row about them."

Even so, Rab noticed that as Aunt Lucy turned away, there were tears in her eyes.

High in the tower at St. Grimelda's, there was a surprise for Emmaline. A good surprise. The kind she had almost forgotten could exist anymore. A parcel was lying on the floor. It was the package she had seen someone carrying away from the storage shed. The package that Rab had smuggled into the school this morning.

"It was left outside the equipment room door with a note addressed to us," said Josie. "Read it!"

Emmaline tore open the envelope, and scanned the lines excitedly.

Dear Emmaline and Josie,

I took the liberty of bringing this parcel to you, rather than allow it to remain in the place your confederate chose to secrete it. I felt that the chances of it falling into the hands of those who would wish you ill were rather too strong, as there are a number of people — teachers and pupils — who are watching your every action with considerable suspicion. In particular, your classmate Amelia and her cohorts can be assumed to be keeping you under close surveillance. It is not in their interest for you to show signs of independent thought and action. Their own power comes from keeping the school in obedience to Mrs. Wackett. Today's events involving Princess Purnah will no doubt bring even closer scrutiny of your conduct. I personally wish you well and hope that, whatever your intentions are, your efforts prove successful. I cannot at this time reveal my identity, but perhaps that circumstance will alter. I trust this parcel contains useful materials for your plans.

Sincerely,
A Well-Wisher

"This is very odd," said Emmaline in wonderment.

"I dunno exactly what it means," said Josie. "Lots of long words. What's a 'confederate,' then?"

"A helper or an ally, I suppose."

"'Cohorts'?"

"Er, like soldiers, I believe."

"'Scrutiny'? 'Surveillance'? 'Secrete'?"

"This isn't a vocabulary test, Josie! What matters is that we have the package, and we also have a friend we didn't know about."

"Enemies, too, by the sound of it. But we already knew about them. Open the parcel, then!" Josie was eager to move ahead.

The box had been packed to fit a lot of things inside it. Aunt Lucy's work, no doubt. There was glue, scissors and brushes, a ball of string and a large piece of canvas. There was a bundle of fine wooden strips, each about two feet in length. There was a map of the area with a route marked from the school, over the cliffs and into the sea, where a little boat was drawn. In tiny handwriting, Aunt Lucy had copied Sir George Cayley's notes, the ones Emmaline had used to build the first two flyers, onto small sheets of paper. There was a silk lungi — a turban — from Lal Singh that could be used for any number of useful things. There was an odd sort of apparatus that seemed to be a lifejacket with a propeller on the back and pockets for sandwiches and a copy of *Punch* (included) to pass the time while awaiting rescue. There was even a box of fireworks. All of this was explained in a letter, written in part by Aunt Lucy and in part by Professor Bellbuckle.

The girls started to work right away. Josie was happy to cut where Emmaline told her to cut and glue where she said to glue. Emmaline knew that she was not building the original Cayley flyer (which would have taken too long and

been too big to build, or hide, or get out of the room) but was taking Rab's kite and turning it into an emergency rescue flyer. All it had to do was get her out of the school and a few hundred yards away in safety. Was that a lot to ask? Of course it was. But she had to try or she'd be imprisoned at St. Grim's until she turned eighteen, or perhaps twenty-one, or died of misery and Everglue's Spicy Condimental Sauce ("None More Sticky").

The hours ticked by, and the pair worked ceaselessly by candlelight. The room stank of glue, and their hands were tired from twisting string and cutting canvas.

Emmaline's brow was furrowed with worry. Somehow the flyer didn't seem strong enough. Josie was examining the frame of the flying machine as it came together. "Those bits of wooden strip don't look very tough."

She was right. They didn't. The lengths of wood had been chosen to fit into the box and be carried, rather than anything else. Otherwise Rubberbones would have had to make several trips with materials, and that had been out of the question.

"Well, how about a couple of hockey sticks, then?" suggested Josie.

Emmaline thought it was a terrific idea. "But won't you get into trouble for letting me take them?" she asked.

"I think I'm going to be in so much trouble already that a couple of old hockey sticks won't make any difference, don't you?"

Emmaline was quiet for a moment. "You know, I'd take you with me but, well —"

"I'm not exactly a fairy princess," finished Josie cheerily. "And the kite will only carry a small person. I know that. But even if it was a huge machine that could carry ten people, I'm not sure I'd go with you, Emmaline."

"You wouldn't?" Emmaline gaped in astonishment.

"I don't think so. I really don't have a place to go to. My parents are both dead, grandparents as well. I've got a horribly strict and unpleasant aunt in Wimbledon who is just as bad as Wackett. When I turn eighteen next year I come into a bit of money — not a lot, but enough. The Church Missionary Society became my legal guardian after Mum and Dad died in Africa. I could train as a missionary or a nurse if I wanted to. Or become a governess. I like little ones. So, I do have something to look forward to. And Wackett and Matron might try to punish me, but it doesn't really work, does it? I mean, I don't care what they do, and they've no answer to that."

Emmaline hugged her friend, and Josie, in return, flung the smaller girl to the floor using her best Ball Game skills, and knelt on her chest. "It's great to have a real friend," she said with a chortle.

"You're breaking my ribs," replied Emmaline.

"Oh, yeah, sorry," said Josie. "Prob'ly not a good idea."

Rubberbones was kicking his heels around the cottage yard. He was growing even more worried about Emmaline now. He was frustrated that there seemed to be little he could do to help. And he was upset about that odd foreign girl, Purnah. He liked her spirit — even if she insisted on calling him "Errand Boy." It was discouraging that he'd made two new friends, both of whom could possibly have been eaten by pterodactyls. (What were the odds of that?)

Stanley seemed subdued, sniffing around the corners in a pathetic fashion. Aunt Lucy had already gone back to the hotel with Lal Singh, but Rab insisted on staying. He hoped that Professor Bellbuckle would suddenly come up with something *scientific* (possibly involving explosives) that would solve all their problems. Rab would help as much as he could. He thought he might have a knack for explosives. The professor said he could sleep under his workbench if he liked. So Rubberbones wrapped himself in a blanket with the dog snuggled down beside him. Perhaps tomorrow would turn out better.

CHAPTER 29

The Professor Helps Out

"The teachers are smiling," said Hannah. "I don't think that's a good sign."

It was morning assembly. Emmaline hadn't been paying attention. She was exhausted after staying up late working on the flyer. Eventually they had decided that enough was enough, and that the glue had to dry properly before they could work anymore. Josie had carefully placed the kite inside the big cupboard with all the tools and bits and bobs. She'd doused the candles and opened the window wide to air out the smell of glue. Still, if anyone searched, there'd be questions to answer. Emmaline had sneaked back to the dorm, but sleep had not come easily.

Matron and Miss Sharpelbow sat glumly, bruises and bandages plainly showing. But Mrs. Wackett bounded onto the platform before the assembled girls. She was almost grinning. Emmaline knew that there were several expressions that the Wicked Wackett was capable of — anger, suspicion, fury and straightforward evil being the obvious ones — but that grin was not a good sign. Emmaline had never witnessed Wackett grinning before. It was not a pretty sight. Then she remembered. Princess Purnah. The return of the pterodactyls. The hunched body gripped in the talons. She'd seen it, but chances were that none of the other pupils knew. Unless they, too, had been staring out of windows long after lights-out.

"Good morning, gels! What a beautiful morning!" Mrs.

Wackett positively bounced on the wooden platform. She glowed with pleasure. The platform groaned under her weight.

There was a mumbling noise from the gathering, as if the whole audience was stunned into tongue-tied confusion by the sight of a happy Wackett.

"Yesterday was a very busy day here at St. Grimelda's, as you'll recall. Princess Purnah, a pupil here for the past three years, was suddenly abducted. Possibly by agents of a foreign power, enemies of the country. Completely against her will, of course. A terrible surprise as she was happily crossing the quad on the way to change classes."

There was another mumble, and many girls just stared in disbelief. This was not the way anyone remembered yesterday's events at all.

"However, you will all be pleased to know that school staff were able to rescue the princess from her captors, bravely pursuing and bringing her back. A great relief to everyone. While, as we all know, Princess Purnah has never learned to speak a word of English in all her years at this school, she made it clear — by hand signals, pencil drawings and that sort of thing — that she was immensely grateful to be saved from her kidnappers. Of course, she was very shaken up, so she will be in seclusion in the infirmary for a day or so. I shall pass on everyone's best wishes for her complete and rapid recovery. To celebrate her return, you can all wear hats and overcoats to bed tonight. But" — she glowered suddenly — "don't any of you even think of being *abducted against your will*, or there'll be unpleasant consequences!"

Emmaline breathed a sigh of relief — Purnah was safe, even if she'd been carried off by the pterodactyls. Around her the girls simply appeared numb, unable to decide what to think or feel.

"I also need to tell you that a servant at this school was acting as a spy for the foreign agents, passing messages and that sort of thing. She has been dismissed, naturally. I'm sure that none of you will mind taking on her duties as part of your kitchen chores."

Emmaline suddenly remembered the note in the bottle of sauce. As she wondered if it had been found, she felt Matron's sharp eyes — one of them black — boring into her. They were watching, indeed.

"Get up, Robert! I have something to show you!" shouted Professor Bellbuckle.

Rab clambered to his feet. Stanley was yipping in his happy, interested sort of way. He'd forgotten all about being sad. That was yesterday. Rab wished he could feel the same way.

"This doohickey here is going to be a big help," said the professor.

He gestured toward a tube cut in half, like a shallow trough. It had some form of telescopic sighting instrument set on a cog on a wheel on a brass thingamajig. It aimed upward and could pivot to change the direction it faced.

"What is it?' asked Rubberbones.

"This is the Bellbuckle Aerial Defence Rocket Directional Device, Mark I. I made it this morning while you were still asleep."

"What does it do?"

"It is designed to shoot down those horrific creatures we met last night. To wound them grievously, so they fall from the skies. Or, at least, to scare 'em up pretty darn good."

Rab was impressed. But he did have a question. "Couldn't you just shoot at them with a rifle or a shotgun?"

Professor Bellbuckle looked down his long nose, through his glasses. Clearly this was not what he wanted to hear.

"No rifle has been designed to bring down those monsters.

Didn't you tell me that your friend the colonel shot one of 'em yesterday? And yet, last night, there were clearly two of the creatures flying over our cottage. No, the problem clearly calls for rocketry."

Rab was about to say that Colonel Grimble-Boare had struck the beast with the sort of light shot that hunters used for pheasants. Indeed, he'd sworn that the pterodactyl was simply a very large crow. But he held his tongue. The professor's fondness for fireworks made him include them in every invention he could.

Professor Bellbuckle looked at him a bit more kindly. "Besides, I don't much like guns. I almost shot three toes off once."

"You nearly shot your own foot?" asked Rubberbones.

"No, I nearly shot my older brother's foot. That was what caused the trouble between us. He's held it against me ever since, and that's been forty years," said Professor Bellbuckle.

Rab thought that if the professor's aim was so bad,

perhaps he shouldn't be shooting off rockets. But, again, he didn't say so.

———⋙◦⋘———

Emmaline wanted nothing more than to get through the day so that she could see how the flyer would look once all the glue was dry. If she and Josie could at least put the pieces together, she would be happy. She'd hook the kite onto her shoulders and make sure that the big new wing and the smaller rear wing (made with two hockey sticks and a panel of stretched canvas) would fit in position. Of course, the next stage would be the really difficult part; having a flying machine set up inside a building was all well and good, but the real point was to be able to fly. Still, first things first.

It didn't take long for Emmaline to realize that Amelia and her cronies were watching her. They were quite subtle about it; they didn't point or stare, but every time she looked up, Amelia or Gwendolyn or one of the twins was observing her. Once Petronella hissed at Petunia for being a bit too obvious about it, which made it more obvious still.

After dinner, Amelia made it clear. "Listen, Cayley. Listen well. We know you are up to something. We'll find out what it is. I told you when you got here that it is in your best interests to follow the rules. You'll be punished if you don't. Clearly you have not understood that lesson. My friends and I are not about to suffer because of your foolishness — we've already got extra chores because of that stupid woman losing her job! So, be warned!"

It was an impressive speech, as if she had practiced it, which Emmaline thought she probably had. Amelia was the sort who wanted to be the queen of all she surveyed, even if she was really just chief toady to the Wicked Wackett.

Emmaline's first instinct was to tell Amelia what she could do, where she could go and what she could shove in her mouth at the same time. She'd done that with great gusto only yesterday. But being tremendously rude had only got her sent to the Black Tower when she tried it on Wackett and Matron. Amelia couldn't lock her up, but this was no time to bring bad things down on herself.

She smiled sweetly. "I am sure you know best, Amelia."

***

Lal Singh was talking to an old harbor salt when Rab, Professor Bellbuckle and Stanley reached the dock. The Sikh had selected a small, old-fashioned steam launch with paddle wheels. It looked as if it might have been somebody's weekend pleasure boat — about forty years ago. It was twenty feet long with a torn canvas awning. The paintwork was faded and peeling, but the engine was well oiled. When the owner started it up, the old boat purred like a satisfied cat.

"Bit shabby, but runs good," said the man, a ruddy-faced old seaman in gumboots and an ancient blue jacket.

Lal Singh bowed slightly, and the professor stepped aboard with Rab and Stanley following on his heels. Nipping at his heels, in Stanley's case.

Professor Bellbuckle addressed the old sailor. "How much for this here fine vessel?"

The sailor named a price. Lal Singh, behind him, gestured that it was too much. Rab suspected that Lal Singh could persuade him to bring the price down by half; Lal Singh didn't say a lot, but what he did say was always right.

The professor didn't seem to notice what the Sikh was try -ing to tell him. "Sold!" he exclaimed, pressing a crumpled wad of banknotes into the sailor's hands. Some of them were English, others had interesting colors and designs that might have been from anywhere. Rab had never seen so many different kinds of money, or as much. He was used to copper pennies and the occasional silver sixpence or shilling.

"I can never get used to paper money," explained the professor. "Silver dollars is what I understand."

The old sailor seemed perfectly happy to get used to Professor Bellbuckle's paper money, and it took Lal Singh's quiet intervention to sort out the correct amount of legal British currency. The boatyard owner would have been happy to take the rest and see if the bank would accept it, but Lal Singh wouldn't allow it. Professor Bellbuckle knew nothing about the value of money. Even Rab could see that.

"You could have 'ired the boat for a few days," he said. "You didn't 'ave to spend all that money to buy it."

"Aha, my young friend! If I hire the boat, I have to return it in the same condition as I took it. Which is all right for some people. I, however, plan to make modifications to this fine seagoing vessel. First off, I need to try out my Patent Locomotive Elixir in the engine. Just a few drops will give her a turn of speed that'll fair astound you, my boy. Run like a racehorse! And then I'll make mechanical improvements. A mount for the rocket launcher, of course. Maybe some cartwheels under the boat to make her truly amphibious. I'll work all day and all night! We'll call her the *Savannah*, after my beautiful home city."

Rab couldn't help but notice that Lal Singh was quietly rolling his eyes at the professor.

Before they left, Lal Singh had a few words with the boatyard man, who agreed that the price paid had included use of a shed, a ramp and a berth at the quay.

The professor had a gleam in his eye.

Emmaline was scrubbing away at the pots and pans as part of her punishment. She also had to go through all the buckets of food slops with her fingers in search of lost pencils or buttons, a particularly nasty task; so far she'd found a penny and a set of false teeth, unclaimed by anyone. Madame De Gauloise was supervising in her flighty "excuse-me-a-moment-*mes-chéries*" sort of way.

Gwendolyn, Amelia's hefty henchwoman, came in with a tray of cups and plates.

"Madame says you're to go up to the infirmary and fetch Princess Purnah's tray. Bring it down and add it to the pile of crockery to wash." She had a rough, throaty sort of voice. Emmaline realized she'd never actually heard Gwendolyn speak before. All she'd been aware of was threatening silence and the cracking of knuckles.

"How do I know you aren't just making that up to get out of doing it yourself?"

The big girl glowered at Emmaline. "Oh, no. I have to run an errand. No. I'm sure that the princess will be happy to see you."

"Odd thing to say," thought Emmaline. But she wasn't going to argue about it. She set down a soup tureen that she'd been told to scrape with her fingernails to remove month-old turtle innards (Mrs. Wackett liked turtle soup) and went off up the four flights of stairs to the infirmary. Emmaline had never been there before. Who in their right mind thought sick people needed to walk up eighty-nine stairs?

Emmaline knocked on the door. Nobody answered. She pushed it open. There, in a narrow bed, lay Princess Purnah, apparently uninjured.

"I've come for your tray," said Emmaline, conscious that the girl would not understand her words. But there was no tray to be seen. Emmaline frowned. The princess looked at her, eyes widening. Then she did something that she had never done at St. Grimelda's. She spoke in English. Very quietly.

"You is Emmaline Cayley, yes? No? Yes?"

Emmaline took a sharp intake of breath. "Er, yes, I am."

"You friendings with Errand Boy Rab, Lal Singh, Aunty Lucy, yes?"

"Er, that's right."

"You will be escapings much soonish, am I not rightly in this matter?"

Emmaline was completely taken aback by this turn of events. Of course she knew that Rubberbones had come to Princess Purnah's aid when she made her escape. That must have been a huge surprise to the princess and to Rab himself. But Emmaline hadn't thought what it all meant. She was still having trouble with the idea that this small, dark girl who had never spoken a word since coming to St. Grimelda's spoke English at all.

"Escaping? How do you mean escaping?" asked Emmaline. She was trying to sound innocent.

"Emmaline Cayley, I is with you. I am speakings with your family and friends and I wishes only to be much helpful, as I am needish helping in my own escapings. You is buildings a flying machine, am I not rightly in this?" Purnah's eyes flashed.

"Flying machine? How can I be building a flying machine?" Emmaline opened her hands wide in the universal "What, me?" gesture.

"Oh, porok! Oh trustings me do. Is Errand Boy Rab's kite, whats he mysteriousish flies in. You be buildings it again. I wishings help. I wishings escape." Purnah smacked her hand down on the bed cover.

"Look, even if I had a flyer — and I am not saying I do, mind — it would hardly be able to carry two people, would it? I'd love to help, but —"

"You mistakes me. Glekk! I not wish to ridings in kite. I sick of flyings! I is carried through air by horridly monster birds, big claws, many fierce scratchings. Only safes because of whalebone corsetly underthingies. Flyings! Trikk!" Princess Purnah spat, which is not what well-brought-up young ladies do.

"Oh," said Emmaline. "Well, what then?"

"I helpish you in you escapings. You helpish me."

"If I can. But I'm not sure how." Emmaline was interested now. Perhaps it wasn't such an insane notion after all. Purnah was clearly much more than she had appeared.

"We decidings that when times is coming about. Now, you be goings before all suspicions is arousings upon your head. Remembers, I saying nothings for I speakish none English, as you is recollecting. This is importants, for foul enemies all arounding us."

"Enemies?" said Emmaline, startled. What had "a well-wisher" said about that? "Which enemies are you thinking of?"

"Always muchly enemies. I is daughter of famous Mir of Chiligrit. Always enemies — in palace and in schoolings. Rememberish what we Chiligritis saying: 'Strangle or be strangled!' Is favorite proverb."

With that valuable thought in mind, Emmaline went toward the stairs. She stopped at the door. "I was supposed to take your tray down."

"Oh, golly, yes," said Princess Purnah. "That Gwendolyn girl did that, befores you comes in."

Emmaline thought about that, in confusion, as she climbed down the eighty-nine steps.

CHAPTER 30

Fireworks

That night after everyone had gone to bed, Emmaline and Josie took the newly rebuilt kite out of the closet. Emmaline had decided to risk charges of indecency by wearing only a pair of long-legged knickers (St. Grim's regulation underwear for young ladies) and a black jersey sweater. She had rubber-soled shoes and had pinned her hair back from her face. If she was going to be catapulted into the sea from a great height, sensible clothes were very important. She couldn't swim in a dress and corsets.

Over her sweater Emmaline had fastened Professor Bellbuckle's patent inflatable life preserver. She had decided to do without the sandwiches (now stale) and the copy of *Punch*. (The professor had not included the gin or cigars that he would have offered other potential rescue-ees. Even the professor knew that fourteen-year-old girls don't need gin and cigars.)

The kite was ready. It was really one large, batlike wing made of canvas on a framework of wooden struts, with a harness of straps (made from the padded leg guards that Miss Sharpelbow refused to let the girls use since they were too prissy for her taste) to hold Emmaline safely in position. Josie made Emmaline stand in the middle of the equipment room, arms outstretched, then brought the kite up behind her.

"Hang on while I get the straps over your shoulders," said Josie. "Stop wriggling or I'll have to tie it on with that turban thingy." The lungi was much longer than Emmaline had expected. It was made of a tight, fine silk and rolled out to be fifty feet long. She thought of it as one more of those mysterious things about Lal Singh that could not be explained. Perhaps he was a secret agent of some kind; he might have throwing knives concealed in his pointy Indian slippers, for all she knew.

Emmaline did not want to be tied in by the turban. They'd only just attached a couple of extra straps that would keep her safely fastened to the kite and, besides, if the thing went crashing into the North Sea as expected, she didn't want to be tied down underneath the wings in case she couldn't release herself. That wasn't a welcome thought.

"Can we get the tail-feather bit on, too?" asked Emmaline. They couldn't; the room was far too small. Those pieces would have to be tied into place at the last minute on the roof. Emmaline and Josie could assemble only the main wing and the carrying harness, holding the contraption

sideways at an angle to fit into the corners of the equipment room. It was "blinkin' inconvenient," as Josie observed.

"I wish I had some goggles," said Emmaline.

"Yeah, goggles'd be good," agreed Josie. "Blimey, you look the complete birdwoman. Are you sure the wings don't have to flap?"

"No, they don't flap," replied Emmaline confidently. "That's a complete misunderstanding about the principles of flight as they apply to the human form —"

Josie, of course, had no idea about the principles of flight. This was no time for a lecture on the science of aeronautics.

"Tell you what, Em. Let's plan on tomorrow night for your escape. We'll climb onto the roof of the main building under cover of darkness, then launch you off when the dawn comes up around six or six-thirty. Depends on the weather an' all, of course. How soon do we have to send the fireworks up to let 'em know?"

Emmaline checked the small selection of fireworks that Professor Bellbuckle had included in the parcel along with the following note:

> *White one, twenty-four hours' notice. Golden one, an hour or two beforehand. Green one at time of departure. Red one in case of warning, postponement, cancellation. Small ones, use for self-defense — they shoot the durn-tooting-est fireballs this side of China, yessiree!*

"That's all good, then," said Josie. "We need to sneak up onto the roof anyway, just to make sure it can be done. Let's do that and send up the white firework."

The two girls had been on midnight adventures around and above the school before. Emmaline wriggled out of the kite straps, and the pair slipped warily out of the window and across the roof. Josie set the rocket in the gap between two slates, angling it up toward the ridge. "Nice, very nice," she murmured as Emmaline lit a match and they watched the flame sizzle along the fuse. The white rocket whooshed high to burst in the sky over Fishwick. Josie stifled a chortle as they beat a silent retreat across the rooftop.

"Good rocket, eh, Emmaline! Like Elijah and his flaming chariot!"

Emmaline blinked, uncomprehending. "Old Testament, Em," chuckled Josie. "Book of Kings. I am a missionary's daughter, you remember."

It was past midnight and the boy was staring out of the window of the professor's cottage. The school loomed black against the midnight-blue sky. Rubberbones knew that Professor Bellbuckle would want to do something madly scientific to the boat, like hack it into pieces and put it back together again so that it would be four inches longer and run on railway tracks and have its own telephone system. Rab knew this was because the professor was *a genius*. But Emmaline was going to need a rescue vessel soon. Having a fantastic machine ready in five years' time wasn't any good if you needed it now. He had heard Aunt Lucy talking with the professor about it.

"Ozymandias, dear, I know you are upset about the princess and those terrible creatures — what did you call them? Terry-somethings? But we must trust in Emmaline's common sense and ingenuity. You've sent her the maps and the instructions and the life-preserver. She's got everything she asked for to build the flyer — at least, we hope she does. We'll just have to wait."

"Lucy, my dear, I am just not certain about that boat. It's as old as the Blue Ridge Mountains. I'd hate for Emmaline to land in the sea and have those gosh-darn monsters attack her before we arrive at the scene."

"Anything is possible, but you said that the boat had a good engine, even if everything else is a bit shabby. Lal Singh knows what's important; I can always trust him to make the best choice."

"Yes, but —"

"I know. There are faster boats in the world, but not one here at this moment. I'm sure you could build a wonderful, amazing rescue racer. But we need a boat *now*," said Aunt Lucy firmly.

"All right, all right, Lucy. No revolving machine guns. No phosphorescent searchlights. No amphibious ski-wheel-skates with retracting whatchama-callits."

Rab's attention was suddenly caught by a flash in the sky. "Miss Aunt Lucy! Professor Bellbuckle! It's a firework!"

The professor rushed to the window to catch the dying drops of white fire falling from the heavens. "By criminy, it's the white rocket! We are up for tomorrow night!"

CHAPTER 31

Fog Over Fishwick

Something was wrong. Emmaline knew it as soon as she got up the next morning. A layer of thick fog sat over St. Grimelda's like one of the school's cheap gray blankets. This was exactly what she didn't want. She needed a gentle breeze to take her out to sea, not a windless day of shroudlike mist. Without wind she wasn't going anywhere; even if she somehow got the flyer to lift off, the fog would prevent her from seeing a thing. "Calm down, Emmaline," she told herself. "If it's not tonight, another chance will come." She'd send up the red firework to postpone the flight, then send up another white one when the weather turned again.

But something else was going on. She noticed at breakfast. Amelia and her friends were watching more intently than before. There was whispering, with hard looks in Emmaline's direction. Then she saw something that stopped her heart.

Petronella was fishing something out of a bottle of Everglue's Spicy Condimental Sauce. Something that Mr. Everglue never intended to be in a bottle of his estimable sauce. A soggy piece of paper.

Emmaline tried not to stare. Was the note still readable? Was her name there to be seen by anyone? Or had Mr. Everglue's unique blend of fruits and spices destroyed the evidence against her?

An hour later, she knew. The headmistress had called an

emergency assembly. There was to be some kind of announcement. The schoolgirls filed into Big School, most hushed, some whispering.

Mrs. Wackett was drawn up in her most imposing, threatening posture on the platform, her hands gripping the podium so tightly that Emmaline almost expected it to scream for mercy.

"Gels, it is clear that someone or some*ones* are involved in misconduct of the worst kind. The details do not concern you at this time. There is to be a thorough search of the school for evidence of this . . . this *nefarious* scheme. Only trustworthy girls selected by teachers will assist. The rest of you will return to your classrooms and remain there until I give the order for you to resume your normal activities."

Emmaline thought that there was an evil glint in the headmistress's eye — and she could have sworn that it was directed straight at her.

The fog hovered like thick soup over the little harborfront of Fishwick. Lal Singh was readying the *Savannah*. If it had been up to him, he would have named it after his own hometown, a village on the River Sutlej in the Punjab, where his brothers had worked on boats of all kinds. Rubberbones knew this from the evenings he had spent talking with Lal Singh. The butler had opened up in the boy's company and told marvelous tales. You'd never know that the silent Sikh could talk so much — or that he knew so much about seafaring.

"All ready, my young friend. Coal, water, provisions, oilskin capes and hats. A rope for rescuings. Miss Lucy will be bringing some food, no doubt, so I have made arrangements for myself and anyone else who dislikes earthworms in their

dieting. The professor will doubtless be along with some of his inventings at any moment."

And he was. Professor Bellbuckle had a rocket tube, all gleaming brass and cardboard and a set of lamps arranged on hangers in the form of the letter *E*. "For Miss Emmaline, so she'll know it's her target for landing if it's dark," he explained. "We'll set this up in the prow. Or the bow. The pointy bit. The front part of the boat, anyhow," said the professor. Lal Singh smiled and only rolled his eyes a little bit at Rab.

The Sikh butler-turned-sailor put his hand up to feel for a breeze. "This fog concerns me, for it is most thick, sitting over this land like a great toad on a rock. But perhaps it will lift. Perhaps a wind will arise to blow it out to sea. It is not in our hands to control the powers of nature."

Emmaline sat stiffly in her seat. What should she do? She could hope that the search would be limited to the girls' lockers and storage trunks and that nobody would go through the equipment room. Or that, somehow, no one would recognize what the kite was. It could be some strange old piece of sports gear locked away in a closet. It was possible, wasn't it?

"Don't be stupid," Emmaline thought to herself. "Miss Sharpelbow will be going through her own stores, not someone like Amelia or her cronies."

She looked up to see the teachers picking their pets to help in the search. Of course, Amelia and Gwendolyn and Petunia and Petronella were selected and some girls from other years who were their exact copies. Nasty, sneaky teachers' pets —

And Josie. Miss Sharpelbow had taken Josie by the arm. Because she was a suspect? Or because she was captain of games? Not because she'd betrayed her friend, though. Emmaline knew that.

What to do? Run? But where to? To the equipment room and try to get the flyer out somehow and then — do what? Two people were needed just to get the harness and wings in place. And then what? Climb out of the window and jump off the roof hoping for a freakish and miraculous updraft of wind to lift her into the fog and away? "Ridiculous," thought Emmaline.

The girls were leaving Big School row by row. Emmaline's next class was drawing with the scatterbrained Miss Silverspoon (since Miss Chalkfruit had gone to buy pencils last week — and never came back). Or would Miss Silverspoon be searching, too? Surely not. The teacher couldn't find a present under a Christmas tree. Emmaline racked her brain.

Should she pretend to be calm and see what happened next or make a bolt for it?

As her fellow classmates walked in a group through the hallways, Emmaline noticed that she was being watched. Miss Scantcommon, at the far end of the hallway, was observing her with an icy stare. She was the rebellious girl. The suspicious girl. The Cayley girl.

The whole class seemed perturbed. Emmaline had assumed that she was the only one who might be afraid if the school was searched, but all the other girls seemed just as worried. Some were passing notes to one another once they got to their seats. The always-silent Anna wrote note after note to the always-crying Margaret. Bernadette was the only pupil who even bothered to pick up her pencil in an effort to draw; she made bold and angry markings that looked nothing like the inoffensive bowl of fruit Miss Silverspoon had placed before them. Hannah was whispering to anyone who was willing to be whispered to. Miss Silverspoon wrung her hands as if it was all a terrible thing, and began crooning a little lullaby to keep herself calm.

Emmaline realized that everyone had something to hide. Amelia and her cronies were on the side of Wackett and her staff, trying to find out all those secrets, whatever they might be. That was their strength. They found out secrets and used them against the other girls. Everyone had secrets at St. Grimelda's, because nothing was allowed and all joy was strictly forbidden.

The clock ticked. Everyone fidgeted quietly. Each girl was waiting for her secrets to be discovered. Emmaline wondered if they were *all* going to the Black Tower this afternoon.

Then she heard it. Everyone heard it. Miss Sharpelbow had a very loud, very clear voice, as games teachers are supposed to, and it carried easily down the corridor.

"Josie! The door is locked. Let me in!"

The bell rang to end the class. Nobody could remember if Mrs. Wackett had said whether the girls were to stay in one classroom or go to their next lesson. Miss Silverspoon ceased her little song and looked even more frightened and confused than usual. Were the girls leaving or staying until told otherwise? Emmaline wasn't about to ask.

She was out of the door in a flash. Josie must have locked Miss Sharpelbow out of the equipment room. If there was a moment for action, this was it. Emmaline had no idea what that action should be, but it was time for it anyway.

"Where do you think you're going?" someone hissed behind her, grabbing her by the shoulder.

It was Gwendolyn. Big, knuckle-cracking Gwendolyn. Amelia's henchgirl. "I've come to fetch you. This way, and hurry up about it!"

"Let me go, you big bully!" shouted Emmaline as she tried to twist free.

"You've got it all wrong — I'm here to help you escape!" Gwendolyn's voice was gruff and her words were unexpected. "*I'm* your well-wisher, you know."

Emmaline gawped. "*You!* Never!"

"Let's not discuss that right now. Josie says I'm to get you up on the roof as quick as I can."

Gwendolyn set off at a sharp pace, up the steps to the infirmary. "Purnah's in on it, too. Did you know she speaks English? Came as a complete surprise to me."

Emmaline shook her head in shocked disbelief, but followed Gwendolyn. What were her other choices?

Gwendolyn heaved open the infirmary door to reveal Princess Purnah — up, dressed and armed with a sharpened butter knife. "I kill them all if they try to stop Emmaline Cayley escaping. I cut out they lungs and they gizzards, too. Swish, swish! Glekk!!"

Emmaline was touched by the princess's loyalty but would

have preferred her not to wave the knife around quite so enthusiastically.

Between the three of them, they quickly pulled a heavy iron bed in front of the infirmary door. "That should hold 'em off for a few minutes," said Gwendolyn. "Quick now. Out the window and up onto the roof. It's not a hard climb."

"You've climbed it, then?" asked Emmaline hopefully.

"Well ... er ... no. But I'll help boost you up."

Purnah was already out of the window. "Porok! Me girl of mountain kingdom. Chiligriti princess. Climb like Himalayan goat." Then she was gone, shinnying up a drainpipe. Emmaline took a deep breath and followed.

"Don't look down," she told herself. "You've climbed up and down the roof and the tower before. But that was with Josie — in the dark. Nothing to see if you looked down. Not like now —"

"There she is!" It was a girl's voice coming from the quad. Petunia? Petronella? "There's two of them!"

Emmaline looked down. A dizzying feeling surged through her. A hand reached down and steadied her. Purnah. Below, in the quad, a gaggle of girls were pointing upward. The tall, thin figure of Miss Scantcommon bustled across the courtyard to see what they were looking at, then raced back toward the staircase in pursuit as she realized what was happening.

"Isn't a picture to be looking at," growled Purnah close to Emmaline's ear. "Up on roof, now!"

Gwendolyn's head appeared from the infirmary window below. She was waving a fist, pantomime fashion. "Oh, you naughty girls! Come back and let me collar you!" Her voice was loud enough to carry across the yard. From below, she must have seemed like a baffled pursuer.

The two girls were now up on the roof. The fog was thinning out into patches of mist. Princess Purnah ran (very

much like a Himalayan mountain goat) toward the tower.
There was a figure at a window above. Josie. She was lowering
something out of the window. It was the kite, hanging from
Lal Singh's amazingly long silk lungi.

"Get this untied and I'll drop the wings down next," Josie
called out in the loudest whisper Emmaline had ever heard.
Princess Purnah was tugging at the knot, her eyes bright
and a bit savage. Having a sharpened butter knife certainly
brought out her Chiligriti mountain heritage. Josie pulled
up the lungi; a few moments later she was lowering the wings
and then the tail piece. All the time there was a thumping noise,
and the voice of Miss Sharpelbow demanding to be let in.

"I think the lock's jammed, miss!" shouted Josie. "You
might want to send down to the village for a locksmith. I'm
trying to open it on this side!"

Emmaline was struggling into the Bellbuckle Mark-
whatever-it-was lifesaving jacket, then pulling on the straps
that held the kite to her back. This was all madness! The
sky was brightening, true, but there was still hardly a breeze.
The maps were in the equipment room and, to be honest,
she'd got so caught up in the confusion that she wasn't sure
which way she was facing. Where was the North Sea,
anyway? Oh, there it was —

Princess Purnah was behind her with the newly made
wing and the stabilizer fashioned from hockey sticks and
canvas. She had a ball of string and her knife. "I strappings
you up goodish, Emmaline Cayley. I pushes you off roofs if
you are liking it. Can I has this lungi?"

Emmaline wasn't going to argue about the lungi. She
wasn't going to argue about anything with a mad girl from
a wild country she had never heard of, brandishing a butter
knife. "My gift to you, Princess Purnah."

"That's 'Your Highness,' please, Emmaline Cayley."

There was a blast from the equipment room window. A

firework. The one that meant Emmaline would be leaving in an hour. Then another firework — a spectacular Roman candle affair that burst high up in the air. The one that said she'd be leaving right now. "Can't remember which is which," Josie said, grinning. "Best do both right now."

Emmaline looked at Princess Purnah as she tightened the cords that held the kite. The wind was whipping the princess's hair across her face as she tied the knots. The wind —

The wind that was blowing out eastward across the North Sea! "This must be some sort of divine intervention," thought Emmaline. Josie, the missionary's daughter, would have seen it as God lending a helping hand.

"Stop right there!" a voice bellowed from behind Emmaline. It was Miss Scantcommon. She appeared, advancing relentlessly across the roof. She must have followed them up somehow. Through the infirmary window? Or another way? It didn't really matter. She'd got them.

Almost, that is. A figure suddenly careened into the schoolmistress, knocking her onto the slates and pinning her down. Gwendolyn! "Sorry, Matron, didn't see you there. Wasn't looking where I was going."

Princess Purnah's eyes flashed. "Maybe I cuts her gizzard out. Maybe not. But you go, Emmaline Cayley. You go now."

She smiled and scrambled away. Emmaline adjusted her wings. She gazed into the eastern horizon. She took a deep breath and looked along the fifteen paces of tile that would take her to the edge. She had to do it. Why was it so difficult? Why was her chest so tight and her throat so raw? Was she the girl who couldn't fly — or the girl who could?

She might have paused a bit longer, but Princess Purnah gave her an almighty shove to get her started.

She was running forward. She was running into nothing. She was flying.

CHAPTER 32

Time to Fly

"I do believe the fog is lifting some," declared Professor Bellbuckle. Stanley barked in agreement. Aunt Lucy was unpacking the dogcart and paying a small boy to stable the horse for the rest of the day.

"Do you think Emmaline will attempt her escape in the daytime or wait until after dark?' she asked.

"I'd want to come under daylight, ma'am, if I had the choice, less'n she can see in the dark like a raccoon. Of course, it depends on a lot of things. Depends on taking her chance when she can," replied the professor.

"Well, I shouldn't want her to miss her lessons."

That *did* sound a bit stupid, even to Aunt Lucy as she said it. When you are trying to escape from a horrible school where students are treated like prisoners, it seems rather silly to worry about getting a "B" on your chemistry test. Not that they even taught chemistry to girls at St. Grimelda's.

There was a flash above the cliffs. Rab saw it first. "Firework!"

"The golden one!" exclaimed Professor Bellbuckle. "So, let's be ready for her to make her attempt within the next hour or two!"

A second flash came within seconds. A burst of green against the sky, muted by the fog, but clear enough. Professor Bellbuckle's fireworks were better than the ones sold in shops. More vivid. More powerful. They were among the reasons he was no longer welcome in several European countries.

"Er ... make that any minute!" he added. "Gosh darn it! That's much too soon!"

Lal Singh said softly, "It looks like Miss Emmaline must leave in a very great hurry. We should be in position as soon as can possibly be done."

Aunt Lucy jumped down into the boat, pulling the hamper of food with her. "Cast off, Lal Singh! Belay the forrard jib, hoist the fo'c'sle, aye, aye, me lads, and off we go!"

Emmaline's feet kept on running for a moment before she understood that they weren't touching the roof. The breeze came from behind, buffeting the canvas of the main wing and pushing her out across the edge of the cliffs. Below her, the ground dropped away. There were rocks and the sea lapping around them in white swirls.

"Good-bye, Em! Good luck!"

Emmaline smiled. She couldn't turn around to see, but she knew the voice. Josie.

"Good-bye, Josie!" she yelled back in her loudest voice. "Good-bye and thanks! One day —"

One day they'd meet again, when they were both free. Now Emmaline was free of the insane rules and bullying authority, and all the things that told her that what she wanted was wrong. That she had to be someone else.

If only she made it to safety.

Emmaline held her arms out straight and continued to sail through the air. She had to. There was no means of steering. She remembered how Rubberbones was able to make the kite go wherever he wanted, by moving his arms and legs. But she hadn't the slightest idea how to do that. The kite had no real controls at all. Perhaps the old Gypsy woman, Madame

ZaZa, was right: Rab had some magical power of flight.

She would keep on going until she landed in the sea. Hopefully. It seemed like the best place to crash.

———

"Can you make it go faster, Lal Singh?" asked Aunt Lucy as she anxiously surveyed the sky.

"It is a boat, memsahib. It begins slow, it gains speed, it becomes slow again over a distance. It is not like a horse. It does not gallop." He seemed, well, tetchy. Irritated. He didn't normally talk like that to Aunt Lucy. If Lal Singh was worried, Rab knew to be worried too.

The little craft puttered forward out of the tiny, cramped harbor of Fishwick. Its docks and wharves and jetties were designed for the trawling vessels to unload their catch. There was a stone breakwater, ages old, built to keep the fierce North Sea from lashing upon the moored fishing boats; just getting out of the harbor involved maneuvering to and fro. Rab knew that boats couldn't get up to top speed very quickly; and when they did, they couldn't stop very easily, either. It had to do with moving through water — "friction" or "traction" or something like that. What you didn't want to do was slam into a pier or another boat. This was what Lal Singh was trying to avoid, and what Professor Bellbuckle didn't seem to care about.

"I have this elixir I made up," he pleaded with Aunt Lucy, "I can pour it into the cylinders and make the boat go a hundred miles an hour!"

"You'd blow us up," she replied.

"Well, at least we'd be able to swim to safety, seeing as how it's taking us all day to get out of this danged harbor!"

Rab hated to hear them quarrel. He knew it was all about Emmaline and their shared fear that they wouldn't arrive in time when she needed them.

Stanley started yapping and bouncing up and down. He was pointing toward the school, like the hunting dog that one of his ancestors must have been. Rab scanned to see what had made Stanley so excited. The mist had lifted almost completely. The towers of St. Grimelda's loomed above the village, frowning down from the top of the cliffs. He saw a movement. Something flying. It could be a bird or a bat or even one of those hideous creatures that had taken Princess Purnah. But it didn't fly like any of those. It looked like his kite. Which meant it was —

"Emmaline! Look! It's Miss Emmaline!" He began frantically waving his arms.

Lal Singh held his hand up to shield his eyes from the weak sunlight. His vision was superb.

"Yes, indeed it is Miss Emmaline. But I fear we must make ever such better speed, because I see those pterodactyls also." Stanley saw them as well, and growled menacingly in their direction. Still they came on.

———◦◦◦———

Emmaline soared through the sky. The wind was holding her up, gusting forward, then letting her descend in little sweeping steps. She felt wonderful. She felt fearless! All the terrible things that she'd imagined were nothing more than bad dreams. Flying was magnificent. She knew now why Rab liked it so much. She was like a great bird herself, arms outstretched as the mists parted and evaporated before her. Below she could see the span of the coast of England as it fell away to the gray, cold sea. The little harbor of Fishwick was over to her right, but she couldn't see a boat anywhere.

"Come on, Aunt Lucy," she whispered. "Come on, Lal Singh, come on, Rab. Be there for me when I splash into the water. Otherwise," she thought, "I shall be cold and wet, and I am still wearing a long black skirt and sensible shoes, and the kind of underwear that explains why ladies faint at difficult moments. And this life preserver seems awfully *experimental* —"

Emmaline was looking for difficulties ahead — in the choppy, dark waters below. She didn't realize that the danger was behind her ...

... until she heard the sound. The terrible chittering of the pterodactyls. They were calling to each other, and they were in hot pursuit of her. Whoever had released them had been quick about it. Mrs. Wackett herself? That cold intelligence that set the Wicked Wackett apart from her underlings was what made the headmistress so formidable an enemy. Miss

Sharpelbow had been outwitted by her favorite pupil, Matron had been felled by a diving schoolgirl, but the headmistress was not to be beaten so easily. The birds were flying again, and they were in their own element. It was not like the feeding at the Black Tower. There they had been caged; here they could swoop.

"You think too much!" said Emmaline to herself. All she could do was hang on and hope for the best.

She heard the beating of wings and the scream that sounded like a battle cry. The pterodactyls were approaching fast. In a moment, they'd be on her.

———

"Pass the matches and be quick about it!" snapped Professor Bellbuckle. He had set up the rocket launcher by means of clamps and handles. It was a bizarre-looking contraption of shiny brass and cast-iron pieces, all around a battered cardboard tube that had come from a roll of carpet. A very large rocket on a stick protruded from the open upper end.

Rab passed the matches. The professor lit one, touched the fuse and stood back as a satisfying fizz flickered up the coil of cord. The whooshing sound was equally satisfying. The Bellbuckle Anti-Dirigible Rocket, Mark XII (built for shooting enemy balloons — if the enemy had any — in time of war), certainly made a powerful impression. It hurtled upward, zigging to the left and zagging to the right, then exploded in an impressive display of many-colored fury.

Unfortunately, it didn't blow up close to the pterodactyls. Nowhere near. Closer to Scotland, probably.

Rubberbones stared intently at the sky. Emmaline was floating nicely, and the craft seemed to have excellent lift. She'd done well in fixing his old kite. Although she didn't seem to know how to steer it. The kite didn't have any controls, so you had to sort of wriggle in the air to move the bits of canvas in the directions you wanted. Rab couldn't explain it at all; he just knew how to do it.

The terrible monster birds were coming on something fierce. They'd have to act fast. Rab handed another rocket to the professor.

"WHOOOOOSH!" Once again the rocket tore upward, turning like a corkscrew and exploding in the direction of Norway.

"Think soothing thoughts, Emmaline!" shouted Aunt Lucy. "Think of kittens and bunnies and, I don't know, spiders. Lizards!"

Lal Singh was at the helm, trying to keep a steady course to help the professor's aim as much as possible. (Rab thought that the professor needed a lot of help with his aim.) The Sikh's piercing eyes scanned all around as he held the wheel.

"Look! An explosion at the school!" he shouted.

Rubberbones turned just in time to see a brilliant flash, then a cloud. Smoke was rising from the Black Tower. Stanley was barking furiously.

"Did I hit the school?" asked Professor Bellbuckle. He was quite excited by the idea of actually hitting something.

Aunt Lucy did not share in his enthusiasm. "Just because the headmistress is a horrible ogre and the teachers are cruel beasts is no reason to set the school on fire. Think of the poor schoolgirls, Ozymandias!"

"Quick! Fire again!" yelled Rab. "The birds have got Emmaline!"

———

Emmaline could feel the blow as the first pterodactyl speared its talons into the newly made upper wing. There was a sharp pulling across her chest as the straps were stretched tight; the creature was trying to grab on to the wing and seize it. There was a sound of fabric ripping. The craft lurched forward. Suddenly she was twenty feet closer to the sea.

As the first pterodactyl shredded the canvas of the big wing, its companion wheeled around in a great circle to the front of the flyer. Emmaline locked eyes with the hideous creature, straight on. Its eyes were cold. Reptilian. Evil. Its teeth were like daggers in the huge open jaws, and the razor-sharp talons were thrust forward to attack. The creature hovered, then dipped into a dive. All at once Emmaline realized what it was going to do. She felt terror jolt through the pit of her stomach. The beast's head lifted suddenly, and the dive became a steep climb toward the underbelly of the glider. It sped directly onward, aiming at the girl so oddly attached to cloth and string and wood.

"Steady on, Emmaline," she said to herself, trying to drown out the sound of her rapidly beating heart. "Remember the Ball Game." And, remembering the Ball Game, and her many practices with Josie, she did what she had to. Her arms were stretched and useless — she could not duck or weave — so she swung back her right leg and, with all her might, kicked the pterodactyl square in the throat.

"Gwoarrkk! Aarghkk!" the creature cried, and sheered off to the left. It sounded like Princess Purnah's native tongue, as spoken by a shocked and surprised dinosaur.

"Take that — you nasty, filthy beast!" shouted Emmaline, because she knew that was exactly what Josie would say.

She looked down. The flyer was falling, a foot at a time. She could see a small boat below, moving quite fast, with a trail of smoke arcing above it. She could see figures aboard. Was that Rab? Was that Aunt Lucy? Surely that was Lal Singh?!

Another horrible ripping sound. The pterodactyl seemed to be tearing the main wing away, one piece at a time. Emmaline felt helplessness surge through her once more. If only she were closer to the water. She must be a hundred feet up. Too high for a plunge! The crash would kill her, just as if she

were to land on cobblestones. Suddenly she thought of the house at Lower Owlthwaite, Aunt Lucy's horrible food, Rab's trust in her, and her friendship with Lal Singh and Josie. The joy of these wonderful memories far outweighed the prospect of dying in St. Grimelda's uniform underwear.

Emmaline was jerked out of her thoughts by a loud BANG behind her. The pterodactyl she had kicked just a moment ago flew back into her line of vision. There was another BANG! The beast jerked, and fell sideways toward the water.

"There is a man on the cliffs with a shotgun," observed Lal Singh as if this were quite normal. "He has wounded one of those flying creatures quite grievously, I should think."

Rubberbones tore his eyes from the flailing, falling monster and looked at the top of the cliff. "It's the colonel! The man who helped the first time them birds got 'old of the princess. He shot one then, but it didn't seem to hurt it much."

Aunt Lucy still had her eyes locked on Emmaline. "I expect he's using heavier ammunition this time. I suggested he might when I sent him a note this morning. More soothing thoughts, Emmaline!"

"Lucy, my dear — you did what?" The professor turned to her in astonishment, almost setting a match to his shirt cuff rather than the next rocket he had prepared.

"I sent a note up to Colonel Grimble-Boare at Wisteria House. I told him that the huge crows that had bothered the young lady the other day might be flying today, and that he was invited to shoot at them if he liked."

And at that very moment, the pterodactyl plunged into the sea.

CHAPTER 33

Fire and Water

The other pterodactyl was as determined as ever. It was continuing to rip the wing apart, strut by strut. Emmaline hoped desperately that the kite would hold for another minute. Thirty seconds. Just enough for her to get closer to the water. The sea was gray, it was turbulent, it was as cold as Mrs. Wackett's heart, but it was still water rather than hard ground.

Emmaline tried to remain calm and concentrate. But that was easier said than done. She tried to think about the science of flying and controlling the glider's response to updrafts and — it was no good! The main strap that held the stabilizers in place was torn away. The craft was going down —

The big wing tore away with a jolt. Emmaline spun to her left, then right, then fell forward. The original kite was still holding, and a gust caught her as she fell. She could see a ball of flame below, and a trail of something that hissed and burned swept past her.

There was an explosion, much too close, and a burst of fire raining down all around. For a few moments Emmaline was stunned by the sound and the bright burning light; then she saw the gray waters hurtling toward her. Too quickly for comfort. But the kite was suddenly flaming around her, and it seemed a very good time to be in the water. There was a rush as the flames were extinguished, and Emmaline was plunged into the freezing sea. Spluttering, with wreckage wrapped around her, she came up for air. Rubberbones was holding a rope so far over the side of the *Savannah* that he almost fell in himself, until Lal Singh caught him. Stanley was yapping, and a tall man Emmaline didn't recognize was waving madly. "Hello, dear!" called out Aunt Lucy. "I'm making tea!" Lal Singh's strong hands tore the sodden canvas aside and pulled Emmaline up into the boat.

"It's my nicest turnip tea — with a dash of honey and cod-liver oil," said Aunt Lucy, putting the steaming mug in Emmaline's shivering hands. "Drink as much as you like. It's nice and hot!"

Emmaline was cold and wet and extremely grateful to be alive. All the same, the cup of hot liquid smelled pretty foul. She grimaced. "Er ... thanks, Aunt Lucy."

The boat was puttering back into the little harbor at Fishwick. Aunt Lucy had wrapped Emmaline in warm blankets, and Stanley had licked her face. Lal Singh smiled like a muscular saint.

"Thank you as well, Lal Singh," said Emmaline.

"You are mostly welcome," he replied.

Rab had simply looked at Emmaline with huge, little-brother eyes until she wondered if there was something he wasn't telling her.

"Is there something wrong with my face?" She wondered if it had been burned, or scarred, or horribly disfigured somehow. It was certainly damp, and her hair hung in wet strings.

"Oh, no, Miss Em. I'm just happy to see you again," said the boy.

Professor Bellbuckle introduced himself with a great flourish, and kissed Emmaline's hand. She wasn't used to that and she almost giggled. He was in high spirits after his last rocket had, according to him, "Shot that rascal pterodactyl right between the eyes. Saw him fall dead with smoke and flame all around him. It was like the battle of Chickamauga back in sixty-three with the Yankees up on Snodgrass Hill —"

Aunt Lucy did not want to hear about the battle of Chickamauga; she doubted that the professor had been anywhere near the place, at least in 1863. He might have been to look at the monuments since then. He was a sweet man, but, really, his imagination did run away with him at times, and she didn't want to encourage his tall tales.

"Ozymandias, dear, you hit the wing of the *flying machine* and set it on fire. The pterodactyl flew away, and a jolly good thing, too. You can't just kill things at your own convenience."

"That colonel fella did!"

"Well, perhaps. But the bird was probably just injured. Anyway, I don't want you firing rockets at living creatures like that again. It isn't good for your soul."

Professor Bellbuckle was about to retort that *rockets* were good for his soul, but just then Rubberbones caught everyone's attention.

"That tower at the school! The black 'un. It's definitely on fire!"

———

They were gathered in the cluttered parlor at Professor Bellbuckle's cottage. Emmaline was dressed in fresh, dry clothing that Aunt Lucy had brought for her. She had told her story at tremendous length and in exact detail. Everyone had insisted, Stanley included.

"What about Josie?" asked Aunt Lucy. "Won't she be in trouble?"

"Yes, I'm certain she will. I wanted her to escape with me, but she refused. She said that she was going to stay at the school until her eighteenth birthday, which isn't far away now. She'll be in trouble for locking the door on Miss

Sharpelbow — that was quite clever, wasn't it? And for shooting off fireworks, too. And they'll suspect that she had something to do with the flying machine. But really, Josie doesn't care what they say or do. They have her actual, physical body locked up at St. Grimelda's, but Josie is as free as anything in creation. She taught me to fight monsters."

"Why did the girl — Gwendolyn, was it? Why did Gwendolyn help you? Wasn't she one of Amelia's friends?" asked Aunt Lucy.

"Yes, and I don't know. I wouldn't have guessed that she was my well-wisher at all. I'd stopped her from being rather badly thumped by Josie one day when we were playing the Ball Game. Perhaps it was that. Or perhaps she was just tired of being Amelia's flunky."

"What ever will become of Princess Purnah? She wanted to escape. She did escape — until the pterodactyls came back." Aunt Lucy was clearly upset even talking about it.

"She was very brave. A bit — very brave," said Emmaline, remembering the wild expression and the sharpened butter knife.

"What about the pterodactyls?' asked the professor. "No school should have pterodactyls. It's just plain wrong."

Emmaline didn't have an answer to that, though she agreed, obviously.

There was the sound of a horse's hooves and iron-tired wheels outside the cottage door. The brass knocker clattered against the woodwork.

"Hullo there! Anyone at home?" It was a man's voice, fruity and deep.

Aunt Lucy answered the door. "Why, you must be Colonel Grimble-Boare! How are you? I saw that you received my note this morning, then?"

"Yes, indeed, dear lady. And a fine day it was! Shot one of

those blighters, y'know. Big crows! Gray! Not like normal crows. Big as a —" The colonel was not entirely sure what the crows were as big as.

"Big as pterodactyls," thought Emmaline. Who was this old man, anyway?

"Well, I lost it when it went down in the water. Can't get the dog to swim out after a bird when it's gone into the sea. Probably not worth it anyway — can't eat 'em, what what?"

Rubberbones nudged Emmaline. "This is the gent as saved Princess Purnah an' me when them teachers was chasing the grocer's van. Gave us tea and cakes, too. Good cakes." Emmaline was glad to see that Rab's perspective on what was important had not changed at all.

"Anyway, I'd have been here earlier but the roads were clogged with the fire engines trying to get up the hill to that girls' school. Part of it was on fire, y'know. The headmistress wouldn't let 'em in, so they all came down again. Odd woman!"

"I understand that she is very strange," agreed Aunt Lucy. "She doesn't like intruders, even when the place is on fire."

"By the by, I have someone to see you. That's why I came in my carriage. Wanted to make sure everything was all right before we went ahead. A bit shy of crows, y'know."

He opened the door of the coach. Princess Purnah leaped out, her eyes glistening.

"Parek! I am here! Freed once again! Hello, all! Hello, Errand Boy! Hello, Emmaline Cayley!"

She went straight into the cottage (the courtyard reminded her of the birds).

"How did you get away?" asked Emmaline in astonishment.

"Aha! Excellent tale! Gives me cake, I will tell!"

Evidently she shared Rubberbones's taste for sticky sweet things. Aunt Lucy brought out cake made of cabbage and pickled rhubarb. "Porok! Glekk!" said the princess, as she tasted a piece and threw it over her shoulder in disgust. She began to tell her story.

"When you is escaping, Emmaline, Matron leaps up. I ready to cut her spleen out with butter knife, as good Chiligriti princess know to do from babyhood. She take off down staircase I know nothing of before. I turns to Josie, who is at window with fireworkings, and I says to her, I says, 'Josie, give me rest of rockets and matchlings.' I already have excellent silk lungi you gives me. Josie throw these rocketses and matchlings down to me. Now she can be telling horrid Sharpelbow that door mysteriousish stuck, oho, she not knowing how, no evidences what prove Josie parts of your escapings, Emmaline Cay-lee. I runs down staircase and comes out facing Black Tower. Wicked Wackett comes out of tower door and talks with Matron, keeping door open. She bin up loosing birds, no doubt. I see 'em fly. They evil teacherwomen not see me. They look other way all time, oh yes! I creeps through door, sneaky-sneaky like mountain jackal. Still not see me. Wackett and Matron angry, say many bad words! I go up tower, remember birds' lair since they catching me. Horrid birds. I get vengeance! Tringg! Vengeance excellent for Chiligriti princess! Birds gone out, when come home, they findings no home. Ha, ha!"

Emmaline was trying to follow the turns of the story. Princess Purnah had many good points, and was very resourceful and brave. She was also a bloodthirsty lunatic. Perhaps that was what they taught you as a member of the royal family in Chiligrit.

"So, I ties fine silk lungi around battlement. Very long, but I thinking, 'Is long enough, then?' But I Chiligriti princess, and learning to fall down ravines for fun when just a toddling-child. Is Chiligriti way — we getting no toys like English childs, has to play on mountains. I puts fireworkings in nasty birds' bed of straw. I lights fuse of big rocket and sticks it in food bucket so not fly about, but splutter sparks all over straw. Ho, ho, how I laughs! I laughs loud! I laughs too loud, perhaps, for Matron come up stairs and catch me, so I —"

Emmaline groaned. Aunt Lucy cried, "You didn't!"

"Cut out her intestines with butter knife? No! Sadly, not enough time for proper knifings. I shoot rocket at her, distance like me to you right now. Ha! Nemek! Skirt catch flame, roll over, fall down stairs! You should see her faces! Excellent! I sets blaze with other fireworkings, see straw catch light, then bounding over the wall and down the lungi to ground. Only drop about twenty, maybe thirty feets. Not far. I roll over, not breaking no bones at all. Errand Boy be happy to see it! Lucky you no try that, Emmaline Cayley! You be all broke in bits! Run along, I sees fine old Colonel Grimblingbore and say, 'Hello, pleased to see you again, good day. I come with you now. Keep gun loaded.'"

Aunt Lucy looked pale. Professor Bellbuckle leaned forward. "Can you tell me more about how the fireworks performed? From a scientific viewpoint?"

CHAPTER 34

A Quiet, Normal Life

Three weeks had gone by since they returned to Aunt Lucy's cottage. The old house at Lower Owlthwaite was full of people again. Lal Singh was once more the perfect butler. Aunt Lucy had decided to take Princess Purnah into her home for the time being. The two girls took quiet country walks, though Emmaline often had to grab Purnah when the princess tried to steal whole flocks of sheep from farmers' fields. They drew pencil sketches, but most of Purnah's artwork featured disturbing acts of bloodshed. Rab had taken Stanley to his grandmother's house to stay, much to the dismay of her elderly cat. Aunt Lucy regretted that the harvesting time for berries and tubers and odd leafy things had passed while they were away. She was forced to order normal food that people enjoy from the village shops. Professor Bellbuckle was considering Aunt Lucy's offer to move his laboratory to the old barn and stables. There was more room there than in the cottage he rented in Fishwick; anyway, his landlord had been asking questions about the number of explosions the professor had set off. It was really just a matter of moving his equipment, and the professor was planning to build a giant steam leviathan on jointed iron legs to do the job. He had sold the boat back to the fellow he'd bought it from for half the price. This was not exactly a bargain for a boat he had owned for less than a week, but Bellbuckle was not good with money. Besides, it was scorched in places.

There was a huge pile of newspapers waiting, both local and London papers. Emmaline read through them. There was a little bit about a fire in the *Yorkshire Post*.

> *A fire was reported at St. Grimelda's School for Girls. Only minor damage occurred, and the services of local fire brigades were not required. No girls or staff were injured in the blaze, which started in a disused part of the building. St. Grimelda's was founded in 1552 and boasts a reputation as "the strictest school in England." Headmistress Malvolia Wackett refused comment to this reporter.*

Emmaline read *The Times* for news about scientific discoveries and inventions, but there wasn't much to report. What she did find out was that there was a looming crisis over the tiny mountain country of Chiligrit. Palace murders, secret dealings with spies, mysterious abductions and other nefarious doings were "a matter of some concern" to the British government. She showed the report to Lal Singh, who looked thoughtful. Aunt Lucy peered almost blindly at the newspaper because she had lost her reading glasses in one of her jars of pickled snails.

Princess Purnah read with glee the reports of who had been assassinated and with anger the reports of which of her relatives had been imprisoned by bandits. These were, apparently, everyday happenings in the Frizzibuttok Mountains. "One day, I go back, conquer, many executings! I swears it!"

Emmaline was glad to be back at the place she most thought of as home — more than tropical Calcutta, more than the fresh Himalayan air of Simla. Certainly more than the stifling world of her mother and the ladies of society. And certainly far more than St. Grimelda's. She had her aunt and her friends and the freedom to do what she really valued. She had built a flying machine, a simple kite, which had let her escape from the prison of St. Grimelda's. She had overcome her caution — her fear — and flown for the first time. Previously, she'd chosen safety over courage. Safety can be a good thing, but, as Emmaline thought to herself, it may prevent you from being brave. Bravery was essential. She'd learned that from Josie and from Rab, who was always brave, even when bravery was, well, fairly stupid.

Rab was not stupid. He was almost indestructible, which helped, of course. But mainly he took risks when risks needed to be taken. Emmaline was glad to be his friend.

Rab came up to the house every day. His grandmother thought that the people up on the hill were completely mad to pay him for doing no proper, regular work. She wasn't complaining about it, though.

Emmaline was happier about Princess Purnah. Away from St. Grimelda's and pterodactyl attacks and that sort of thing, she became much easier to live with. She had a room down the hall from Emmaline. After a week Emmaline stopped worrying about blades, fires and sheep stealing. Purnah began to seem like a nice, normal sort of girl. For a princess from Chiligrit. Still, Emmaline noticed that Lal Singh kept a close eye on the kitchen knives.

Aunt Lucy didn't understand that keeping a lost Eastern princess might cause problems. Lal Singh had suggested, tactfully, that she write to the India Office in London about Purnah, and to Emmaline's mother about her child. It took six weeks for a letter to get to India, though the telegraph system could get a message there the next day. But Aunt Lucy didn't like telegraphs very much — you had to be very brief, and couldn't be chatty even if you wanted to pay for extra words.

Then one day the postman brought two letters. One was from Emmaline's mother. Aunt Lucy read it and passed it on to Emmaline, as she was told not to do under any circumstances.

Dearest Lucinda,

Please forgive the delay in my replying to your letter regarding Emmaline and her education. At first I was displeased, I will admit, that you chose to criticize my choice of schools for my daughter. Then I came to realize that my former friend, Mrs. Bloodless, is a simply appalling woman, and that any suggestion she might make about the proper education for a young lady must be tainted by her dreadful judgment, spoiled opinions and bullying manner. You won't believe what she said at the viceroy's ball only last . . .

It went on in this way. Emmaline realized that her mother had quarreled with Mrs. Bloodless; everything Mrs. Bloodless had ever said, done or suggested, her mother now considered the work of Satan. The important part of the letter came after a pointless account of a picnic where Lady Frumpington-Bothersome had had her hairpiece stolen by monkeys. Emmaline's mother thought monkeys ought not to be allowed to steal hairpieces.

So I have written to the school to ask that you be allowed to bring Emmaline away to your home. Any suggestions that you might have for a more suitable education to raise my rebellious daughter as a proper young lady will be taken as a favor, dear Lucy.

"Right," said Aunt Lucy, who had not mentioned to Mrs. Cayley that her daughter had already escaped from St. Grimelda's. "Emmaline, dear, why don't we ask Professor Bellbuckle if he is interested in becoming your tutor? And Robert and Princess Purnah's as well, of course!"

Which was an excellent idea. Not in all ways, but in some. The other letter, from the India Office, was short and extremely polite. Princess Purnah was indeed the heiress to the throne of the kingdom of Chiligrit. Affairs in Chiligit were matters for this department. An official would come to visit shortly, if it was convenient.

"Too polite," said Aunt Lucy. "There may be trouble. I know these people. Too polite — well, I think this might spell difficulties. I knew I should never have told them about Purnah. We should have changed her name to Aggie McHaggis and pretended she was my niece from Scotland. Purnah looks a bit Scottish, don't you think? No? With a tartan bonnet, perhaps?"

Emmaline heard the sound that night. She could have been wrong. But then Princess Purnah burst into her bedroom in a nightdress — although without sharp metal objects in her hand.

"Did you hear that, O Emmaline Cayley?"

Emmaline listened hard. She heard it again. A long, piercing shriek with no reply in return. Could it be the sound of a single pterodactyl? A monster without its mate?

Then there was another sound. A rush of steam and a tremendous crash. The house shook. Someone was yelling in an American accent.

"Dash it all, Lucy! I wanted to show you the Bellbuckle Steam Carriage, Mark I, as a surprise. I didn't mean to run into your house!"

Aunt Lucy was her usual calm self. "Hello, Ozymandias. I am sure the house will be fine. Let me help you out of the wreckage and we'll make some of my chocolate, gooseberry and cabbage-leaf cocoa. I expect the girls will be awake, so I'll make a big pot for us all."

"Charmed, dear lady. Charmed."

Emmaline smiled and put on her dressing gown and slippers. There was always time for a steaming mug of chocolate, gooseberry and cabbage-leaf cocoa.

A Few Closing Remarks about What's Real, What's Not and Himalayan Mountain Goats

Sir George Cayley was a real live pioneering scientist in the field of aeronautics, and all I've said about him is true (as far as I know — I wasn't around). Emmaline, his young relative in this story, is imaginary. Everyone else is fictional, too. Yorkshire, London, Calcutta and the Himalayas can be found on a map, although Lower Owlthwaite, Fishwick and the wild mountain kingdom of Chiligrit cannot. This is probably a good thing, all in all. And, remember, just because Rubberbones can use an ordinary kite to fly, you really shouldn't try. No, I mean it. Don't expect me to visit you in the hospital.

P.S. No Himalayan mountain goats were harmed during the writing of this story.

ACKNOWLEDGMENTS

Thanks go to Elda Thomas and her daughter, Edan, for pointing me in the direction of Bill Slavin, who then pointed me in the direction of Tara Walker and Kids Can Press. Bill has been a huge, enthusiastic supporter of *The Strictest School in the World*, drawing magnificent illustrations. Tara has been terrific to work with, and has improved the book enormously by her fierce, Purnah-like penciling and savage editing. Thanks also to Bill Powell — a gifted storyteller in his own right — for many suggestions and spottings-of errors, to Matt Kelland, Bruce Pettipas, Bill McGinnis, Lon Weiss, Ed Dillon, Tracy Wimberley, Dennis and Gus McKinney, Howard Fielding, Harry Morris, Bob and Spencer Murch, Rick Young and Loren Dearborn for reading early versions of the story. The kids of Camp Edan — Rhian Thomas, Merle Davis Matthews, Viva Rae Davis Matthews and Eli Kelly — for acting as a focus group of actual youngsters. The Parliament Street Library in Toronto provided a wealth of inspirational books as well as a home for a writers' group that listened to an awful lot of this book as I worked on it — many thanks to Simon, Laurie, Vern, Ruth, Michelle and Susan! Joanne Schwartz gets special credit for encouraging me to write for young people in the first place. Thanks to my parents-in-law, whose generous checks while I was writing this allowed me to avoid becoming the world's oldest illegal busboy. If I've forgotten anyone, well, that's about what they'd expect of me. Aside from all these good people, I want to thank my father for making up stories when I was a child. And I give special thanks to Lori, for putting up with me all these many years.

Coming soon:

MORE MAD MISADVENTURES OF EMMALINE AND RUBBERBONES!

Featuring Her Royal Majesty, Princess Purnah of Chiligrit in

THE FACELESS FIEND

Being the Tale of a Criminal Mastermind, His Masked Minions and a Princess with a Butter Knife, Involving Explosives and a Certain Amount of Pushing and Shoving

In this thrilling follow-up to *The Strictest School in the World*, our friends try to settle down at Aunt Lucy's rambling old home. Yet, within mere pages they are hurled into madcap adventures involving the nefarious schemes of The Faceless Fiend and his Masked Minions. A villainous plot to abduct Princess Purnah twists into wild chases, food fights, rat fights, ridiculous costumes, balloons over London, fat naked ladies, famous fictional detectives, heroic dogs and assorted mayhem, all leading to a hair-raising finale on the newly opened — and *opening* — Tower Bridge.

Princess Purnah commands "Read it ... or else! Porok!"

ADVANCE PRAISE FOR *THE FACELESS FIEND*:

"It were champion!"—Robert "Rubberbones" Burns, aged 12

"I is much fiercely stabbings at mine enemies, oh yess! Glekk!"
                                    —Princess Purnah, aged 13

"I was quite concerned about the whole thing. It could have turned out badly."   —Emmaline Cayley, aged 14